TOMORROW'S NOT PROMISED

2

FLIP SIDE

ROBERT TORRES

GOOD2GO PUBLISHING

TOMORROW'S NOT PROMISED 2
Written by ROBERT TORRES
Cover Design: Davida Baldwin
Typesetter: Mychea
Copyright ©2017 Good2Go Publishing
Published 2017 by Good2Go Publishing
7311 W. Glass Lane • Laveen, AZ 85339
www.good2gopublishing.com
https://twitter.com/good2gobooks
G2G@good2gopublishing.com
www.facebook.com/good2gopublishing
www.instagram.com/good2gopublishing

loyalty	infidelity
culpable	innocent
accomplice	enemy
secluded	involved
honesty	deception
jealousy	trusting
affection	disgust
revenge	pardon
release	incarcerate

Cathy

TOMORROW'S NOT PROMISED

2

FLIP SIDE

A SHORT STORY I RECALL HEARING:

A man died and got to heaven. After a search through the book of life, the angel told him to enter.

"You've led a good life. Welcome to heaven."

As the man stepped in, he noticed a door with his name on it. "Is this my room?"

"No," the angel said, giving no further explanation.

"Hold on. That's my name. What's in the room?" he asked curiously.

"You don't want to know."

"But I do. Am I forbidden from seeing what's in the room?"

"You can look if you wish."

The man opened the door. What he saw was boxes upon boxes. Confused, he asked, "What's in the boxes?"

"In each one of the boxes are things God wanted to give you. But he gave you all the things you asked for. In the end, he never had the time to give you these things."

A simple story with an even simpler explanation. We can't want for ourselves more than God is willing to give us. Before we twist our lips up telling him what we want, let's thank him for what he's given us already and open ourselves up for all he has in store for us. Trust me: your life will be more satisfying.

Enjoy The Flip Side . . .

ONE

"Shhssssh," Carla tried to hush her little sister. At nine years old, she was the oldest of the two. The crate barely touched her leg. Now her sniveling and crying was going to get them busted. She quickly placed her hand over her sister's mouth. Someone, the old lady who she'd seen earlier, no doubt, called out when the crate fell. Now she heard footsteps coming toward them. Usually she would have left her sister at the church where they'd been hiding out for the last week, but some men came in and began to do some work. One of the men might stumble upon her sister, so she brought her along. Figuring they were just moments from being caught, her hunger pains kicked in. She ripped open the large bag of sour cream and onion potato chips that she'd taken off the rack, spilling several of them on the floor. Caring very little about anything other than eating, she grabbed out a handful and stuffed as many in her mouth as she could. "Eat!" she ordered her sister.

Sandra, at age seven, did as she was told. They would get in trouble and be sent back to the Place.

The Place, to Sandra was better than they had now. At least there they'd eat every day and have a bed to sleep in. Still, her heart raced as the sound of footsteps drew closer.

Delores Tucker owned the corner store on 52nd and Market Street in her West Philadelphia neighborhood. It was a mom-and-pop store that her deceased husband started up after his accident in the plant he worked for left him with only his left arm. In the eight years since his death, much to the dismay of her children, Delores kept the store doors open. It wasn't that her children thought at age sixty-four she was too old to work. Their mother, a picture of health, was in better shape than women half her age. Their fear came from the changing neighborhood they were raised in—one which wasn't the same. The thought of a robbery attempt gone terribly wrong, ending the life of the mother they loved so much, generated their fear.

Delores brushed aside such worries as though they were pesky mosquitoes on a hot summer night. Her faith, as it always had been, was in the Lord.

When she locked the front door a little before six (normal closing time), she thought the last customer had left. She took the money out of the cash register just as she heard the noise coming from the back. "Who's there?" she called out. Her ears strained to pick up any more noise. Nothing.

"Shsssssssh."

Now *that* she heard and she got to her feet. She set the money on the counter. With nothing but the Lord as her protector, she headed toward the back of the store. Right inside the entrance to the room was the light switch. She flicked it on. The sight of the two dingy girls stuffing chips into their mouths reminded Delores of a night when she was no more than the age of the girls she was looking at. It was Christmas morning and Delores got up, hoping to be the first one to the gifts. What she came upon was a group of rats eating the meal her mother had prepared. When she flicked on the light that Christmas morning, the rats barely looked up before they continued to devour their holiday meal.

Carla stared defiantly at the old black woman. She knew stealing was wrong, but it had been so long since they'd eaten a thing—at least three days. Surviving on water and the small wafers given out during communion, her stomach cramped from hunger. The woman would call the cops, but at least their bellies would be full. When the light came on, Sandra stopped eating. They still had time before the cops arrived. "Eat," Carla ordered her sister as she pushed chips into her mouth.

The sight was heart wrenching. Tears stung Delores's eyes as she turned and walked out to the front of the store.

Back to the orphanage is how Carla saw it. Surely she'd get in trouble for what she was forced to do a week ago, but she had no choice. They'd understand. She was only a kid. When the old lady left, Carla looked for a door they could run out of, but there was none.

Since the crack epidemic hit the city in 1988, things got progressively worse. Delores noticed the changes, heard of the killings, saw the funeral processions travel up and down the blocks, witnessed the hopelessness and despair, saw the foundation of her community-family dwindle to single-parent households. Boys running around trying to be men. Girls trying to be women. All before their time. And now this. When did it all stop? she wondered. It took only a minute to warm her dinner that was already in the microwave. She planned on eating as her and her daughter, who was running late as usual, went over the inventory for the store. Not wanting to scare the girls, she sat the plate that contained ham, yams, corn, and cornbread on the crate, and backed away to go stand back at the door entrance.

The aroma from the food won out over the chips. Carla dropped the bag of chips and pulled the crate toward them. Picking up the fork, she dug into the yams, blew on them, and held the fork up to her sister's mouth, allowing her to have the first taste.

Delores stood silently, watching the two eat until the food was all gone.

Carla covered her mouth as she began to hiccup. "Thank you," she managed to get out.

Using the tissue she'd taken out of the Kleenex box on the counter by the register, she wiped her eyes and blew her nose. "You are welcome. Let me get you two something to drink." She left, but returned with two Dixie cups of water. She handed one to each girl. Before she had a chance to say anything further, the buzzer over the front door, a security measure her kids installed to inform her that someone had entered the store (as though her eyes were bad), went off. Her ever late daughter had arrived.

Carla heard the buzzer as well. She smiled at the old lady to let her know she wasn't mad at her. "It's okay you called the po-po on us."

She wasn't that old or unfamiliar with the street lingo of the younger generation not to know what the girl was saying.

"I did not call the po-po on you, child. That's my daughter," she informed her.

Mona Tucker was not only the sole girl out of her five children, but she was also the youngest at twenty-five. Her closest sibling was nine years her senior. When she asked her mother, who was thirty-eight at the time she got pregnant, one time if she was planned, Delores told her what she told most people: "Man planned and God planned, and God was the best of planners." It took Mona awhile to grasp her mom's meaning, but eventually she did. Life's lessons came from her mother. Harsh realities are how she often described such fate.

Being a daddy's girl and having four very protective older brothers was the reason for her being spoiled. Also, if you asked Mona, it was the reason for her being single. When she was younger, boys stayed clear of her. Even now she didn't get any date offers—mainly because men thought someone as beautiful and sexy as Mona had to be taken. The others wanted no part of the little sister of the notorious Tucker boys, who not only were tough individually, but had the "fight one, fight all of us" mentally. There were easier females to get after.

Mona saw her mother standing in the doorway to the storage room. She re-locked the front door. "Sorry I'm late," she announced. She had no reason for being late. She just accepted that she always was. Nearing her mother, she could see that she'd been crying. "Mom, what's wrong?" She stepped up beside her mom and could not believe her eyes.

Carla took her sister's hand and pulled her to her feet as she got up as well. "Sorry for stealing, lady." They might've been able to run past the old woman, but knew the daughter could catch them easily.

Mona looked at the empty plate and the open bag of chips, and knew how the scenario had played out. Anyone but her mother finding the two girls would have immediately called the police and allowed the authorities to deal with them. "You caught them back here illegally, eating stolen chips, so you decided to feed them your dinner."

"What else was I supposed to do?" Delores asked.

"Call the cops, maybe," Mona thought to herself, but didn't bother saying. Her eyes and attention went back on the girls. "Hi, young ladies. I'm Mona. What are y'all's names?"

Just briefly Carla thought of not answering her or giving her the wrong names. She figured no harm would come by revealing their names. "I'm Carla, and this is my little sister, Sandra. She doesn't talk."

"Oh, she's deaf." Mona was proficient in sign language, having taken a class in eighth grade to learn it. Now she was a pre-med student at Penn University.

"No, she can hear. She just doesn't talk," Carla explained. "Can we go now?"

Mona saw no reason to detain them. The last thing her mother was going to do was call the police. Yet their dirty appearance had her worried. If they left, where would they go. "Where are y'all going to go?"

The quick answer Carla wanted to spurt out was "home," but she hadn't had a home since the age of five. That was right before the death of her mother. With the exception of staying briefly at two separate aunts' homes for seven months, the two had been wards of the state—once even being split up, but Carla caused so much hell that it was decided that the two would remain together. Any thought of her mother saddened Carla. Her body began to shake, her lip began to quiver, and then the tears came.

Mona dropped down to her knees and engulfed the two crying girls in her arms. She said absolutely nothing. She really didn't know what to say. Nothing in her life's travels had prepared her for such an encounter.

Carla initially fought against the woman's embrace. Being in the orphanage amongst the older and more experienced girls, she learned not to show any weaknesses, not to get attached to the foster families. But the woman smelled so much like her mother, so she fell into the hug.

Delores looked on. She couldn't understand how two small children could reach such a deplorable condition.

The crying died down enough for Mona to ask, "Where are your parents?"

"My mom is dead." Carla had never met her dad

so she had no idea who or where he was.

She hadn't seen her two aunts or her cousins since she and her sister were taken out of their home. She had no family that she knew of. None of the foster families had worked out. Not in white households, black ones, Puerto Rican, or even in the one Chinese family they lived with. The latest one had turned out to be the worst one ever.

For the last week, they'd been hiding out—staying the last four or five days in a church eating the wafers given out during the Sunday communion. Three to four days ago the food ran out and that prompted her decision to go out and steal something for her and her sister to eat.

She had no real plan, just intended on running and hiding for as long as she could. After only a week, Carla was tired of running. Sandra was showing signs of stress, and as the oldest, it was Carla's job to make sure her sister was okay. She looked into the woman's eyes. "He tried to hurt her."

Mona was confused. What was the girl talking about? "Who tried to?" and then it came to her. The story had died down, but the day before while watching the news, an anchor mentioned the disappearance of the two children. A picture had accompanied the story. If you cleaned them up, washed them, it was them. She saw it now.

Recognition spread across her face. "Oh my God!"

The look didn't get by Carla. "He tried to hurt my sister, so I killed him."

What shocked Mona more than the girl's words was the expression on her face when she said them. It was said so matter of fact, no sign of emotion or remorse, that Mona had no doubt the girl's words were true.

"I killed him," she repeated as though no one had heard her the first time.

A week ago the death of a Mt. Airy man, discovered shot in the chest by his wife, had been the top news—especially after it was reported that two black girls they'd opened up their home to as foster parents were now missing.

Mona knew the missing girls now stood in front of her, and the girl's next words sent a chill throughout her body.

"I'd do it again too," she said.

Mona didn't doubt her. Delores began to pray.

"It's going to be okay," Mona said, but her words lacked the same conviction and confidence as the young girl's earlier words.

* * *

For two years, the courts fought to bring Carla Porter to trial. Many thought she was entirely too young to be tried as an adult. Her mental capacity came into question; as did cries (from people) for the young girl who proved ungrateful and a cold-blooded killer to face a murder trial in an adult forum.

Scared and missing her sister immensely, Carla withdrew. The doctors at the psychiatric hospital who interviewed and treated her reported to the courts that Carla was not capable of standing trial and they weren't sure if she'd ever be able to.

The hearing on May 25, 2006 was basically a formality—one in which Carla would be deemed a ward of the state until she was able to stand trial.

After so much time had gone by, the case, which originally generated so much coverage, now nearly went unnoticed.

Carla was brought in wearing her hospital outfit: a shirt and pair of slacks. Her hands were cuffed in front of her, and her chin rested on her chest. An official stood at her side. She met no one's gaze, as her head didn't raise up.

Mona and Delores Tucker were in attendance. Throughout the months, they'd stayed at the girls' side, even trying to get custody of Sandra. Being as though they weren't family, they were being given a hard time. Delores refused to give up on either girl.

"All rise," the bailiff said as the judge came in and took a seat. "In the case of the state versus Carla

Porter, court comes to order."

The judge flipped through some papers on his desk although he knew what he was about to do. "Carla Porter will be remanded in the state hospital until . . ."

"Your Honor," a lady called out, causing those in the room, including the judge, to look at her. She began to walk toward the judge's bench. No introduction was needed, but she said, "I am requesting that I be Ms. Carla Porter's attorney of record."

Judge Steele recognized Libby Rodgers, one of the, if not the, best defense attorneys in the state.

At age thirty-eight and having studied law since graduating from Temple University at age twenty-six, she was feared. A lioness protecting her cubs is how she was described. Every district attorney in the DA's office hated going up against her.

"Ms. Rodgers, the state has already appointed the defendant an attorney."

"Your Honor, I've been hired by the defendant's family."

Judge Steele really did review the papers he had in front of him. He found what he was looking for. "It says here that Ms. Carla Porter is an orphan, Ms. Rodgers."

The courtroom door opened and in walked a woman and two young men—one on each side of her. Tears ran down the faces of all three.

"Your Honor, may I present the sister and two brothers of Carla and Sandra Porter."

All through the exchange between the judge and the woman, Carla had not bothered to look up. But when she heard the words "sister and brothers," she raised her head and turned to look at the three standing there. She didn't know how, but she knew the lady's words were true.

"She looks just like me," India Jones exclaimed. Mindless of everyone in the courtroom, she went to Carla and dropped to her knees. "We are sisters, Carla. My father was your father," she revealed.

For the first time in a very long time, Carla smiled. "Hi, Sister."

India couldn't take it. She hugged her tightly, never wanting to let her go. "I'm going to get you out of there," she promised. By any means necessary, she would.

LaRon and Balil, with tears in their own eyes, went and hugged their little sister. They would not lose her as they had lost their younger brother Derrick. They'd give their own lives first.

Two

India didn't want to leave her little sister. She knew the whole story, getting it from the investigator she had hired to locate the sisters she never knew. With her father having children by different women and then leaving, she was only raised with three of her six siblings. After finding their lost brother Derrick when he was fourteen, they'd only gotten to spend five months with him before he was killed on his fifteenth birthday. Now the long search for the last two remaining siblings was over.

After hearing of her sister's trouble, India immediately hired the best attorney she could. It wasn't a moment too soon. Libby was able to postpone the judge's pending order to put Carla way while she had her own set of doctors evaluate India's sister. Another hearing was scheduled in just a week, at which time Libby intended on not only proving Carla was fit mentally for trial, but also that she shouldn't be held for trial as an adult or juvenile. She was 100 percent positive that within the first week of November, Carla, as well as Sandra, would be with their newfound family. That prediction pleased India, LaRon, and Balil. All three just wanted their little sisters out of the system and back in Pittsburgh with them.

Sandra, still not talking, wasn't as happy to see them as Carla proved to be. After the hearing, the judge granted the siblings a moment alone before Carla was transferred back to the hospital.

"They cut my hair," she announced as she ran her hand through her shortened cut. "Said it would look nice for court."

India just couldn't stop touching her. "It'll grow back and you'll never have to cut it again."

Carla nodded, liking the sound of that. She really didn't like the cut. "Have you guys seen Sandra?"

"We're going to see her as soon as we leave here," LaRon told her.

Her eyes got sad. Her voice lowered as she whispered, "I didn't want to kill him, but he was hurting Sandra. I couldn't let him hurt her."

India began to cry lightly. "I know, baby. I know."

"I had to protect her. I'm the oldest." She stopped and smile. "Oops, I was the oldest."

Indian wiped her eyes and smiled as she hugged her sister. "That's right, Carla. I'm the oldest and it's my job to protect you."

Carla broke the embrace and stared intently into India's eyes. "And Sandra?" "

Yes, her too. When we leave here, we'll be going to see her."

Carla looked at her older siblings and then smiled. "I love y'all." No more needed to be said.

After spending time with Sandra, India found out through Libby how much time and money Delores and Mona Tucker had put out for both of her sisters, and wanted to do something special for them. After calling Libby to get the names and numbers, she called and sat up a meeting.

Delores's prayers had been answered. All she wanted was for both girls to have a chance at life. They weren't out, but after witnessing the courtroom antics the day of Carla's hearing, she was confident that all would be well. She hadn't had the opportunity to talk to the siblings, but was happy they had come into the picture. The morning she got the call from India, she told the young girl that no thanks were necessary, that God placed her where she needed to be, at the time that she needed to be there. "Just a vessel to do his work," was how she phrased it.

She saw no reason why India and her brothers couldn't stop by. She wanted to meet them anyway.

Having witnessed so much negativity and everyone out for themselves, India was refreshed to see what she deemed, back in the day, kind of love. Someone doing something for someone simply out of the goodness in them, or rather the goodness of God in them. Delores or Mona were not gaining anything from supporting her sisters. She learned from the Tucker men that they actually faced people, including members of their church, who didn't support their decision to care for and about her sisters. Some thought a place in hell was awaiting the Tuckers because of their support. Support her sisters they did, though, and for that India wanted to show her appreciation. She came up with the perfect way after talking to Marvis Tucker, the oldest of Delores's children.

"Thank you so much for looking after my sisters," she said to them after hugging Mona and Delores.

Inside the store were all of the Tucker children, along with their wives and children. Delores was shocked to see all of her family. One son had to come in from Atlanta with his family for the surprise reunion. It wasn't that he and his family didn't make the trip twice yearly, it was that it wasn't one of those times.

"How did y'all get here. Why?"

Oliver, his wife, and his three children all pointed at India. Delores turned to look at India, waiting for an explanation.

"I've had an opportunity to talk to your family and people in the community. I was made aware that your caring nature went beyond my little sisters. That for years you've opened up your home, arms, and wallet to perfect strangers—expecting nothing in return and getting even less. I brought your family here today to not only decide who is going to look after the store while you are gone, but also to see you off.

"Gone? See me off?" she said, not fully understanding.

"Between raising your five children, fifteen grandchildren, two greats, and countless neighbors and running a business, it was brought to my attention that you haven't had a vacation since your honeymoon." India reached into her purse and pulled out an envelope. "Africa is a place you always wanted to go. Tomorrow you'll be in Africa."

Delores could not believe it. Her hands shook so much, she was unable to open the envelope. One of her many grandchildren took the envelope and opened it for her. "Oh my," she said as the ticket and crisp one hundred dollar bills were pulled out.

"A little spending money," India said. The counting began, ending at one hundred.

"There's $10,000 here," Aleeka, age sixteen, revealed.

"That should hold you over on your twenty-one-day vacation."

The tears fell. Delores couldn't believe it. Going to Africa was her lifelong dream. What was she supposed to do for twenty-one days? "I can't believe it."

"Your flight leaves at 10:48 p.m. tonight," India said. "Your visa and everything is in the brochure. We really appreciate all you and your daughter Mona have done. Which, by the way, brings us to you, Mona."

Happy for her mother, Mona needed no more than that. She'd always given so much of herself that it was nice seeing someone give her something for a change. Her mother's happiness was truly enough. "You've done something we've been trying to do for years. Get our mom to relax and enjoy life."

"Amen to that," her siblings said, bringing a round of laughter.

After the laughter died down, India turned to Mona. "We heard you are on your way to becoming a doctor."

Mona nodded. Three years more and she'd finally graduate. "Yes."

"You've racked up quite a bit of school loans."

"Loans I'll not be able to pay off until I am an old woman."

"Wrong. Loans that you won't have to pay back," India said.

"The same attorney (for my sisters) is right now handling all your creditors," LaRon spoke for the first time. "You are out of debt and owe no one."

Mona's hands covered her mouth in shock. They couldn't be serious. "I owe well over a hundred grand."

"You owe $134,075, to be exact," India revealed. "It's all going to be paid." Her cell phone rang. She talked briefly and then hung up. She smiled. "It's paid."

Mona nearly fainted. The stress of her debt was cause for worry. She'd not told anyone, but times were tough—tough enough that she really considered dropping out for awhile, obtaining a job, and then returning to school. Now she didn't have to. She couldn't stop crying as she hugged India, LaRon, and Balil.

India felt good. She'd found her sisters. Before it was all over, she'd have custody of them and would return to Pittsburgh. She felt really good. Life was good for her family. The sad thing was, she had no idea what awaited her back in Pittsburgh. It would threaten the very family she loved so much—her own . . .

THREE

Mona couldn't believe the change in the two girls that stood before her. She smiled despite the tears. "Y'all better come back to visit. Mom and I will be very upset if you don't." After finding them in the storage room, the two felt like family now. She hated to see them go, but was glad it was with family.

They stood in the airport terminal moments from them boarding the first plane of their young lives. Surprisingly, neither girl was scared. Both had gained a considerable amount of weight. Sandra still hadn't spoken, but from the look of her smile and the way she clasped India's hand, Mona knew they'd be fine. India already had one of the best therapists waiting to conduct sessions with both girls.

"We'll come see you all the time," Carla said. "And you can come see us."

"Okay."

"Last call for Flight 2207 to Pittsburgh," came the call over the intercom.

"Be good," Mona told both girls before she

hugged them.

"Thanks again, and any time you want to visit, you just let me know," India revealed.

"I'll do that." With one final hug, Mona watched them walk away. Right before they disappeared into the tunnel leading into the plane, they all turned and waved.

"Should've hollered at her," Balil said. At 21, he still didn't have a steady woman.

India liked it that way. Her brother was a student at Pitt University on his way to getting his degree in finance. He had little time for girls, even one as nice and beautiful as Mona.

"Boy, stay focused."

"Yeah, boy," LaRon added. "Besides, that there is a *woman*."

Balil smiled. He knew the difference. His siblings would be shocked to find out he was no longer a virgin. Some things he kept to himself.

"How many nieces and nephews I got again?" Carla asked just as they reached their first-class seats.

"Two and two," Balil said.

She nodded happily. "I'm a little sister and an aunt." She turned to Sandra and said, "You too."

Sandra nodded and smiled. Something lifted from her mind, and for the first time since she witnessed her mother getting strangled by her then boyfriend, her mouth opened to form words to others, "I know," she said.

Balil, LaRon, and India all turned to stare at her, shocked.

Carla wasn't shocked. Her sister always talked to her. It was other people she refused to talk to. She knew her sister was happy, and like her, she felt safe.

* * *

When they stepped into India's condo for the first time, the sisters stared in amazement. "You're rich," Carla pointed out.

"Your big brother LaRon is rich, and any time you need something, you just tell him," India said.

"Like a car?" Carla said.

"A plane?" Sandra countered.

"My own house?" Carla shouted.

"A million dollars?" they yelled as one.

LaRon put both hands on his head and shook it in disbelief. "Yeah, they are our sisters."

India laughed. She'd never been so happy. Well, yes, she had: when she found her little brother Derrick. Three and a half years since his death, it seemed like yesterday. "Want you two to take a quick shower and get dressed. There's some people waiting to meet y'all."

They hurried off.

"Is everything set up?" India asked.

The surprise party welcoming them into the family was set up by Deamber and Denean.

LaRon already got a text saying everything was set up. "It's ready," he said. He had another surprise in store himself—one he shared with no one. Finding his sisters and realizing how lucky he was, and the fact that he was needed, convinced him of two things. He reached into his pocket and pulled out the box that held the four-carat diamond ring he had bought in a Philly jewelry store. He opened the lid for his brother and sister to see.

"It's beautiful." India was happy for her brother. With their third child on the way, it was about time the two got married.

Once their two sisters got dressed, they all left out together. No one took notice of the two cars that had been following them since they left Pittsburgh International Airport.

At the party was Derrick's mother, Jocelyn; her man, George (a.k.a. G); Derrick's two sisters, Rochelle and Tamika; Denean, India's deceased brother's girlfriend and baby's mom; India's nephew Derrick Jr. and niece Derricka; LaRon; his woman, Deamber; and their two kids, LaRon Jr. and

Rontay.

Amber, Denean's best friend was also there, as was Dipset, a nigga LaRon fucked with from St. Clair Village. The reason Dipset was there was the other part of LaRon's surprise.

For years, LaRon and Dip hustled their respected street corners, LaRon on the east and Dip on the south. When one of LaRon's soldiers got robbed and shot, many thought the two separate sides would shed a lot of blood. Under normal circumstances or under different leadership, there may have been killings on both sides. Before LaRon could order retaliation, he got a call from Dip requesting a meeting. What Dip brought to the table was what was taken in drugs and money. As an apology, he also brought $25,000 in cash. The last item he set on the table was his nine.

"You can take what you lost plus this twenty-five stacks as an apology, and have my word no one in my organization will invade your territory again, or we can go to war. Both of us will eventually lose a lot of soldiers and loot. Soldiers, I can replace. Money, I ain't trying to lose. The choice is yours."

LaRon liked the older nigga and the two became business partners and friends from that moment.

Dip had gotten married and stepped away from the game several years back. After suffering a setback, getting robbed, and losing almost $3 million in stash, he went to his longtime friend, LaRon. It was at the right time. LaRon had plans, plans that enabled him to get Dipset back on his feet, while accomplishing his own goals.

"It's not even our birthday," Carla announced for what seemed like the tenth time. Sandra sat silently engrossed with her new cell phone she had gotten.

India noticed how entranced her little sister was with the phone. She had her phone and Carla's phone programmed in no time. "Do you like gadgets, Sandra?"

"Yeah, she's real good with computers," Carla announced. "A geek."

India laughed. "Geeks make the big bucks." She would set her little sister down in front of a computer. She had a matching phone, a Verizon model. Without looking at the directions and having to call a representative, she never would have figured out half its functions. Her sister did it in minutes—on her own.

Sandra nodded without bothering to look up. She was intent on mastering the phone. She didn't know why, but it intrigued her.

Jocelyn looked on at the girls her son hadn't had the opportunity to meet. Dontay, her son's father, hadn't been shit as a man or father, but he sure produced some beautiful children. She wished her son was alive to meet his sisters. She wiped her eyes.

"You okay, Mom?" Denean asked as she stepped up beside Jocelyn, wrapping her arm around her mom's waist.

The party was being held at the recreational center Jocelyn opened with the money her son made off selling drugs, plus money LaRon had pitched in. It was a center bearing his name, right in the heart of the Garfield community he'd grown up in. "I just wish D could've met them."

Denean missed the father of her children and her best friend. Now a freshman in Chatham University, she sometimes found herself daydreaming about what it would be like if he was still alive. They shared a dream of attending college together, raising their kids together, getting married. At times she felt cheated. And then she looked at all they shared, especially bringing two beautiful children into the world. Despite Derrick getting shot and killed on his fifteenth birthday and not getting to see his daughter born, Denean's faith remained. She believed God did everything for a reason, and that Derrick was in heaven with no worries or pain. "He sees them, Mom. He's watching us right now as we speak."

That much Jocelyn believed. Sometimes she just needed a little reminding.

"Excuse me," LaRon said loud enough for everyone to hear him. "We're all here to celebrate us finding our last two lost family members."

A cheer went up from the crowd.

"Finding my little sisters taught me what's really important. It's not money. It ain't a rep in the hoods. Ain't women."

"Better not be women," Deamber interjected. Everyone laughed.

LaRon smiled. "Naw, baby. You the only woman in my life. The only woman I want or need." He paused and walked to the front door. He opened it and people started to walk in.

Deamber looked at her parents, who were no longer together, along with her aunts, uncles, and cousins, in shock. She couldn't figure out why they were all there.

LaRon relocked the door after the last person came through. He made his way slowly toward his woman.

She realized what was going on and began to jump up and down and cry. "Oh my God! Oh my God!"

India grabbed her arm, afraid for the baby in her stomach.

"Yeah, mami , it's that time," LaRon informed her as he got down on one knee. "I wanted your family here to witness this. Deamber, will you do me the honor of becoming my wife?"

Her feet moved a mile a minute as the ring came into view. This was what she'd been waiting for, what she's dreamed about. With her family there, except for her brother Jayson, killed because of his treachery by the hands of the man she looked down upon and answered, "Hell yeah I do!"

The day was perfect. There was only one more major announcement that even caught Dip by surprise.

"Besides getting married, I am also officially out of the game."

This was India's wish for her brother. One she was glad he made before it was too late.

No one realized that it was already too late.

FOUR

After seeing everyone off, LaRon rode with Dip in his Mercedes SL 500. He made the announce-ment, but the excitement of making it died down as they rode.

Dip remained silent. He made the decision to get out of the game six and a half years ago, kinda on the same shit LaRon was on. He had made enough money and he was a married man and a new father. Having witnessed his own dad's dedication to his mom, brothers, and sisters, Dip knew what he had to do. There wasn't anything left for him to gain. He was a millionaire and well-respected nigga who had made it. All he wanted to do was spend time with his family and watch them grow up. In all the years he was involved in the drug game, even as a street-level dealer, no one ever robbed him. Having them niggas put guns to his wife and kid's heads and hear them say they'd kill them all if he didn't open the safe had nearly broken him. Losing the three million hit him hard, depleting his stash considerably. He was glad his family was still alive. It was his woman who told him he was still the head and if he crumbled, they'd soon follow him.

Roger Dipset Underwild had called LaRon. Not only to let him know he was getting back in, but that he needed his help in finding the niggas responsible for robbing him. They had to pay with their lives.

LaRon gave him no directions, simply told him he was going to ride with him. On some real shit, he never thought about this day. Before going to get his sisters, he was considering getting some dope and getting involved in that. Nigga from Africa perping as a jitney driver told him he could get him some pure heroin for three stacks a kilo. LaRon wasn't stupid. He knew how much money he could make from a key of good dope. Buying a few keys was something he was really about to do before his trip to Philly. Now he was out. "I still got niggas out pounding the streets for the fools that disrespected you, fam."

Dip wasn't in touch with the streets like he used to be. The nigga he passed the torch to when he retired from the game, a nigga from Braddock that went by the name of Red, also had his ear to the streets. The niggas that got him would eventually slip up. And when they did, they'd meet his wrath.

"That's good look fam, but real rap. You fittin' to get out?"

LaRon nodded yes. "You told me I'd eventually

get tired of it, get busted, or get knocked. Nigga, I had enough. You sure you want to get back in. I got enough to set you straight without you having to jump back in."

He appreciated the gesture, but he was never the type of nigga to take a handout. From the first stone he ever sold in '90, he'd grinded out of it what he put in. That first time it was off a double-up that he invested fifty dollars on. He still had key fare. If LaRon gave him a good enough price he might be able to snatch up two. "Ain't my style, fam, but appreciate the love. Nigga ain't completely busted."

"Feel that. This shit ain't for me no more. Sittin' on something right. You the right nigga to put on. I know your hustle."

"What you need me to do?"

He had niggas he was going to put on. Jay—his fiancée's dead brother who snaked him by hiring two niggas to take him out, was the closest nigga in his click. LaRon killed the nigga. Dip was a real nigga and he knew he could not only leave him with some of the twenty-two keys he had stashed, but that he could turn him on to his connect. "I got fifteen keys I'm going to put in your hands. Drop me off 150 stacks when you can. After you push it all, get at me and I'll put you in touch with my connect."

Dip hadn't expected this when he left his home

earlier. When he contacted LaRon, he planned on just getting back on for a little while, just enough to make a few dollars. He had a couple properties he was renting out and two stores he owned, so he wasn't on his ass. Hearing LaRon's offer, he knew he was officially back in it, and it wasn't for a minute. This time he was going all out. "Sounds good to me, my nigga."

LaRon took out a key from a hidden compartment on his belt. "Safe deposit box number is 224, at First National."

Dip looked at the nigga like he was crazy. Who stashed cocaine in a bank? "Are you serious?"

"As a heart attack. My people's wife runs the branch in Oakland. Safest place I ever stashed my shit. Take it all out and stash it wherever you want. I'm getting completely out."

Dip took the key out of LaRon's hand. "I got you."

This really didn't feel as bad as he thought it would. Actually, he felt pretty good about it. "Be safe, fam."

The two men clasped hands while they sat at the red light. They didn't see the car across the street from them at the opposing red light. Nor did they see the man in the passenger seat taking several pictures of them.

"Take me back to my ride." LaRon looked forward to going home to be with his family. Truth be told, he looked forward to planning the biggest wedding Pittsburgh had ever witnessed.

"You sure about this?" Dip asked him when he pulled next to LaRon's car.

"Have that shit gone no later than tomorrow before the bank closes."

They gave each other a pound, and LaRon got out of the car and slammed the door. He watched Dip drive off. He stretched and stared up at the sky. When he looked down, he saw the car with two white men in it appearing to be watching him. They drove off. All through the rest of the day, LaRon couldn't get the two men in the car out of his head.

* * *

Det. Clyde Dexter sat alone in his office with the door shut. He'd come through the ranks of the department as he outlined for himself —from a patrolman to detective of narcotics. Now he was the head of an investigation that reportedly stretched as far as Columbia—the biggest drug ring to hit Pittsburgh, Pennsylvania, ever. It was his job to bring them down. He looked at the board of the players that he had assembled. A picture accompanied every name on the board, forty-seven photos in all.

For over a year, his team of men and women, handpicked by himself, watched their targets day and night. So many hours were put in that the mayor stepped in finally and spoke to the chief and told him he wanted arrests, not more investigative work. The chief told him in not so many words to arrest people now. Clyde didn't think he was ready. The man at the top of the pyramid—the head of the drug ring—was still very much a mystery. He had his name and had so many photos of him that the suspect invaded his dreams: LaRon Jones. He wasn't the average drug dealer. His circle was small, and he dealt with so few people directly that it was hard to tie him into the ring. Oh, Dexter knew he was a kingpin, but the evidence he had didn't conclude that. If the mayor would show just a little more patience, he could piece it all together.

Thousands of pictures sat on his desk. He selected one. Picking it up and staring intently at the image, he wondered how all this was going to affect the person in the photo he held in his hands. India Jones, the older sister to LaRon. From all the info his team had gathered, he knew she had nothing to do with the drug ring. But it was her brother he was after. He'd met her at the hospital the night her fifteen-year-old brother was killed. He'd never solved that murder as he had hoped. He wanted to impress her, to bring the killers of her brother to justice. He hadn't. Now, in just a few hours, he'd have to look at her beautiful face again in person as he set the wheels in motion that would lock her brother LaRon up for the rest of his natural life. She'd never forgive him, would never know that he was madly in love with her.

He set the picture down and stood up. Clyde had a job to do. Right then he didn't much like it, but he'd do it. He stuck the cardboard under his arm and walked out of his office down the hall to the conference room. He felt all the eyes on him and had to fight off the urge to smile.

Everyone knew he was handling a major case. It made him feel good. Him, a black child coming up in the projects on the Hill District, raised by his grandmother because his mom OD'd on dope and his dad was a mystery. Clyde had made it up out of the ghetto by hard work and discipline from his grandmom—Nana—that told him early on, "Failing in life isn't an option." As he stepped up in front of all the people waiting on him, Clyde took a deep breath. He'd made it. "Okay, people. This is the day we've all been waiting on."

A loud cheer erupted in the room.

As he looked out at his team, he cracked a smile. This is what he strived for, yet he couldn't help but wonder if India would ever forgive him.

No longer could he worry about that. He began giving out orders, detailing the takedown that would begin at noon that very day.

As he walked into the conference room, Clyde nodded at a man that he would surpass in rank after this major bust. That really mattered very little to Robert Manuel. He had no aspirations of moving further up in rank. Det. Manuel was all about money. He had expensive taste, high-class women, and a gambling problem. He realized long ago that he wasn't going to get rich on a detective's pay. Robbing drug dealers early on had fattened his pockets, but with so much police brutality going on, he'd stopped that. It wasn't long before he came up with a new hustle: leaking confidential info to the bad guys. At first he told local dealers of potential raids, names of informants, and the like. Now he perfected his craft, reporting only to one man who rewarded him nicely. He picked up his phone and dialed the private number. "Mr. Astari, this is that guy. Got some info you might be interested in." He told the quiet man what he knew.

Michael Astari was a business man, the owner of Rock Jungle, where Derrick had lost his life in the parking lot. He was also the head of the Pittsburgh mafia. He'd met the intriguing and beautiful older sister of Derrick, India Jones. He'd never met a woman quite like her, a combination of beauty and deadliness. After helping her get rid of the bodies of the three men responsible for killing her brother, the two remained in contact. Mike made it clear that all she had to do was give the word and he'd get rid of his wife for her.

"And you'd marry me and everyone in the mafia would be okay with that?" she pointed out.

"Fuck them," he often told her, and he meant it. If he could have her, he would easily tell anyone who had a problem with it to go to hell. In fact, he'd send them there himself.

They'd eaten dinner together, caught a few plays, but their nights always ended with a hug, and he'd kiss her on her cheek. Nothing more. That breaking up a happy home shit she told him drove him mad. A time or two he thought about killing his wife so they'd be together. She'd only laugh when he'd tell her his plan of killing his wife.

"Michael, you can't kill the mother of your kids," she'd tell him.

The hell he couldn't. He would kill her and that fuck-up-ass boy she brought into the world as well, who couldn't keep that cocaine out of his nose and caused Mike more headaches than joy.

He knew the type of woman India was, and that impressed him as well. She was all about family. That's why he was so furious with Robert Manuel. Why would he call him only a few hours before the raid? His usefulness had just ended. For his lateness on the news of the raid on the brother of the woman he loved, Manuel was a dead man. First Mike had to warn India. He sat up in bed, waking his wife.

"Honey, what's wrong?"

He ignored her as he punched in the ten digits he knew by memory. "India, it's Michael. You got to warn your brother of a raid the police are about to do at noon." He listened. "Sorry. I just found out myself." She hung up on him and he slammed the receiver back on the cradle.

Sarah Astari had enough of this woman India. He thought she didn't know about her.She had her sources as well. Even had other wives telling her about this black young woman he was out with. Well, it ended now. "I've had enough of this bitch India."

Mike turned in the bed and faced his wife.

"Yeah, I know all about this bitch you've been parading around. When you start dipping your dick in a nigger?"

Mike grabbed his wife by the face, squeezing

her jowls together. "Listen to me, you worthless cunt. Don't ever let a negative word come out your mouth about India again." He pushed her away as she began to cry and he laughed lightly. "You should be bowing to her because she's the only reason why your ass isn't in a coffin."

Sarah looked at him, shocked.

He shook his head. "She won't let me whack you: mother to my kids, wife, all that shit. Won't even let me kiss her. Man, those lips." He let his words die off as he watched her sob uncontrollably. He left her there as he went to shower. All hell was about to break loose in the city.

FIVE

India called her brother immediately on his house phone. She knew enough about sting operations to know her brother's phone was probably tapped. She had to take a chance that his house phone wasn't bugged. "Get on your bike and get the hell outta there now. Lay low and hit me on a new phone ASAP."

She hung up knowing her brother was smart enough to do as he was told. She didn't know if she was part of an investigation. She wasn't dumb enough to get involved in her brother's dealings. It wasn't illegal to have a brother that sold drugs the last time she checked. In her final year of college, she would soon have her law degree. She now did her internship at the public defender's office. It was a madhouse there. After being there just three months, she now saw why so many men, specifically young black men, were in jail. Many didn't prepare or plan for when they got caught. Hiring a private attorney was out of the question.

There was no money for it. No attorney took cars with rims on them, jewelry, or big screen TVs.

And that, India realized, was what a lot of hustlers did with their money. When it came time to hire an attorney, the money came up short, and the woman they left out on the street to handle shit was ill equipped to do so. Hence, the overpopulation of jails and prisons and a caseload that exceeded the public defender staff. So what happened is, many pleaded guilty to their offense. This after seeing their PD once—at the most twice—before their trial.

For India, the work she did was draining, physically as well as emotionally and mentally. Because of the overload of the caseload of the PDs, the attorneys didn't have enough time to properly defend their clients. It was a system that needed an overhaul, but was much bigger than her shoulders could handle. Right now her focus was on her brother. They could come after him, but it would take more than the Pittsburgh Police Department to rip her family apart.

LaRon didn't even take the time to explain to Deamber what was said. He just told her that the call as from India and she told him to get out now.

Deamber hoped it didn't imply what she thought it did. Not when her dream of becoming his wife was about to come true. She sat on the bed and watched him quickly throw on some clothes. She fought off the urge to cry, knowing that she had to be strong. "I love you, LaRon," she told him after she kissed him passionately.

"Everything will be cool, lil mami. Stay positive."

She wanted to ask him what was going on, but after telling her he loved her, he raced out of their bedroom. Deamber stood at the big window and watched him fire off on his motorcycle. The tears finally came.

He rode off, wondering what was in store for him. Until he purchased a new cell and talked to his sister, he would keep it moving. Because he was on point and paranoid as hell, he easily spotted the undercover following him. He was glad his sis told him to get on his bike. He let them follow him as he rode on Penn Avenue, heading toward the parkway. Once he got on 279, heading toward downtown, he opened up the engine on the Kawasaki 1100, reaching speeds up to 160. By the time he got off 279 and crossed over into the Hill District, no one knew where he was. LaRon went straight to one of the nigga's houses he supplied and took one of the nigga's rides. He went straight to the Cricket dealer downtown and purchased a phone.

He made six calls in succession, saying the same thing in each call: "Nigga, it's going to pour and rain like a motherfucker."

In six different houses, crack was being flushed and the houses were set on fire. No evidence would be recovered in those traps. The code he had put into place in case of a situation like this worked to perfection.

He called his sister on his new phone. She answered and called him back immediately on her newly purchased phone.

"They are about to do a major raid involving you."

He figured as much. "Do you know what for or when?"

"At noon is the when. Mike is trying to find out what is going on. He's the one that told me about the sting."

LaRon wasn't too cool with his sis's friendship with Mike. It had nothing to do with the nigga being white. If you let Mike tell it, he wasn't white. Then he'd go on to tell you about Hannibal conquering Italy and how he had black in him. All true Sicilians do, according to Mike Astari. That didn't mean shit to LaRon. She was his sis, and Mike was married. On top of that, he was in the mafia. After she convinced him that she wouldn't get romantically involved with him, he stepped away. Now he was kinda glad she kept in touch with Mike. He looked at his watch. It wasn't quite 9:00.

"Once I find out more, I'll call you on this phone. I'm on my way over to be with Deamber. You hole up somewhere. No driving, and stay off your other phones."

That wasn't going to be a problem. He stomped both of his other phones. "Tell her I love her." He hung up. His sister would handle shit, she always did, but this time he was really scared.

Six

Dip couldn't sleep the entire night, anticipating the time when the bank opened. He wasn't there when the first employee opened its doors, but he was there with Red and two of his right-hand men: a nigga named Joel, who was mixed, having a white mom and black dad; and a nigga named A.D., a nigga that always smiled and seemed to be up to something. Being out of the loop, LaRon had to trust Red's word on the two niggas that Red said came up together on the Westside. With them three, Dip would begin his plan to control the city's drug trade. All he had to do is holla at the nigga Andre from Kirkbrade Street, who was out of the game, to find the one nigga on the North that could lock shit down. All four sides would be his to supply.

Fannie Oliver was the supervisor of the Oakland branch. For years, she'd been dealing with LaRon, so when the four came in requesting access to the boxes in the basement, she had them wait while she tried to contact LaRon. Both his phones went unanswered. She wasn't dumb enough to leave a message. She called India. "Four men are here trying to get in LaRon's box here at the bank."

Initially India though it had to be the cops, but why wouldn't they just flash a warrant. "I'll call you back." She hung up and called her brother.

"If they there, let the nigga get it all out," he told her. He wasn't sure if they knew where he kept his shit. India, Deamber, and Fannie and her husband were the only four that knew the bank was his stash spot.

India called Fannie. She described Dip to her. Fannie located the one she described through her office glass and hung up. "Dip," she said, looking at the man India described.

"That's me."

"LaRon said get everything out quickly and then lay low. He'll get in touch with you."

Dip was never one to waste time with senseless questions. He'd get the shit out and find out what the hell was going on later. "I'll follow you."

They split the keys up amongst themselves, and to be on the safe side, left out at different times. Dip was the last one to leave. The entire exchange took twenty minutes.

Left alone after all four men had left, Fannie said a silent prayer. She had a bad vibe.

She called her husband to check on him. She was relieved that he answered and that he was still home in bed. Whatever bad vibe she had, it didn't involve them. She had no clue that within the hour her world would be turned upside down.

LaRon could do nothing but wait for a call from his sister. He wondered about his money in Altoona. He rarely made the trip out there, but he had no clue what this was all about. The majority of his stash was out there. If he was to guess, he'd estimate close to $10 million. He was tempted to try to get out there to it. He decided to sit and wait on his sister.

India called her brother's attorney and told him to clear his calendar and compile a list of attorneys that could handle the massive sting that would soon be leveled against her brother and his organization.

Hercules Reynolds expected this call a long time ago. He'd been LaRon's attorney since he'd gotten his first gun case at age fourteen. From that moment on, he'd made it his business to keep LaRon out of jail. And up to that point, he'd accomplished that feat. Not only LaRon, but anyone LaRon paid him to defend. He paid well, and that's what led to Hercules and his wife, Marcie, living in luxury. He told India he'd get right on it.

India made it to her brother's home and informed Deamber what was going on. They'd have to wait for more answers, either from Michael, or the police barging in.

* * *

The calls began to come in about the burning houses they had warrants to search. Clyde Dexter knew they had a leak within their department. Their well-orchestrated raid would backfire if they waited until noon. Clyde called a code red over the transmitter radio each unit had. "Carry out warrants now. I repeat, each unit move out now. Security has been breached." As he yelled into his walkie-talkie, he thought about Morgan Freeman in the movie Lean on Me and smiled. He ran through the third-floor office toward the elevator. He was going to lead the invasion into LaRon's home. Now he ordered no one was to exit or enter the home until he got there. He wanted to take LaRon down.

"Sir, the suspect isn't in his home. He rode away on his bike and the tail lost him," came the voice over the walkie-talkie.

Clyde swore and pounded the G button on the elevator panel. All his plans were going to hell. When he found the leak, that person would pay.

"Ain't gonna close no faster if you continue to pound it."

Clyde agreed with Det. Manuel, but he hit it once more for good measure. The door began to close.

"Now, let's just pray it doesn't get stuck,"

Robert Manuel joked.

Clyde didn't see the humor in it. The type of luck he was having, the elevator would crash to the basement and he'd die. The bell sounded and the door opened. He raced off.

Robert smiled. He walked at a leisurely pace. He had a meeting with Michael Astari. It was time to get some gambling money.

India opened the door before the man rang the doorbell. "May I help you?"

Clyde Dexter looked into her eyes. He didn't expect to encounter her. "Ms. Jones," he stated after he got over the shock of seeing her, "I have an arrest warrant for LaRon Jones."

She recognized the cop as soon as he got out of his car and made his way to the door. "Warrant for my brother for what?"

He couldn't keep her piercing gaze, so he looked down at the warrant as though he didn't know all eighty-two charges they had against him. "A lot of charges, Ms. Jones. The most serious of which is operating a criminal enterprise of mass drug distribution." He didn't tell her that a finding of guilt carried a maximum sentence of life in prison. More charges would probably be forthcoming as well. Once the cell doors banged shut, the foundation would begin to crumble and a lot of secrets would be told. That's the way it always went. Plenty would be trying to work out a deal by snitching on the others.

"He's not here."

Clyde looked over her shoulder and saw Deamber, the girlfriend of LaRon. "We also have a warrant to search the entire home."

With the exception of a few crumbs of weed that LaRon may have dropped while rolling a blunt, she knew they wouldn't find shit that was illegal in the house. Her brother wasn't that dumb. His woman and kids laid their heads at that home. She stepped to the side. "Just so you are aware, gentlemen, this home has a very good surveillance system covering every inch of it. Intentional or accidental destruction of any property will make its way to our attorney."

"Ms. Jones, I assure you . . ."

India held up her hand and he stopped talking. "Sergeant Dexter, save the speech. I recall a similar speech awhile ago. You still haven't located the killers of my brother." It was an intentional dig at the man. She'd already handled and disposed of those responsible for killing her brother. The sergeant didn't know that. She turned and walked away from him. She, along with Deamber and the kids, all sat in the living room. India turned on Cartoon Network for the kids. Her blood was boiling.

Clyde turned to his team and said quietly, "Okay, let's do this right people. No fuckups."

For the next four hours, they searched the entire household. Because of his legit business venture, Clyde had no legal cause to evict those in the home and seize it. He stood at the door exhausted. "Ms. Jones."

India slammed the door shut. She didn't have to listen to shit he had to say. She knew the law and her rights. She looked around and smiled. You could barely tell that thirty cops had just ransacked the home. She knew that things wouldn't always go as smoothly as they just did.

Attorney Reynolds called her periodically through the hours they searched the home. She told him there was no need to show up. She had things well in hand. What she needed him to do was keep track of all those that got arrested. She wanted an attorney to be at every single person's side minutes after they were taken into custody. She wanted everyone to know that LaRon wasn't deserting them.

She called her brother as soon as she finished talking to his attorney. "They just finished going through the house. There's a warrant for your arrest."

"I'm going to bounce. Probably make it to Mexico." He'd already planned his escape route. Later Deamber and his children could follow him down there.

"LaRon, listen to me. You are not going to run. It's going to take a lot of money, but we're going to get you a bond."

There were things his sister didn't know. He couldn't take a chance that he'd get out. The last thing he was doing was walking into the Allegheny County Jail.

"They don't have shit. If they did, you would not have any money."

He knew that she was talking about the safe in his Altoona mansion. The home was in his attorney's name. If they knew about it, his lawyer would be arrested as well. He'd have to trust her. "Is Deamber and the kids okay?"

"They're fine. Meet me in front of the courthouse. Your attorney will be there as well. He has more attorneys on this. To get through this, it's going to cost."

He figured as much. "Spend whatever you have to. Move that though." India already had plans on that. "See you in an hour."

If they were to get out of this, she knew that she'd have to outsmart the cops and district attorneys.

* * *

LaRon hugged his sister tightly as he got out of the car. He ignored all the news cameramen and news anchors that lined the street and steps leading to the courthouse.

"I called them, Bro."

He figured that much out.

"Excuse me. My client has nothing to say. Let us through, please."

"Are you going to fight the charges against you, Mr. Jones?"

LaRon looked at the woman like she was crazy.

"Are you a drug kingpin?"

"Have you killed many people?"

The questions continued to come from everyone. LaRon finally made it to the top of the stairs.

"Is your sister involved in this drug ring?"

LaRon ignored his sister tightening her grip on his forearm. His eyes narrowed as he turned around. "Who said that?"

The balding white man who held a small microphone in his right hand raised his left. "I did.

Is your sister involved at all?"

He wouldn't forget the man, and when it was all over, he'd pay with his life.

"Mr. Jones is here to turn himself in to the sheriff's department. He is not guilty of any of the charges brought against him, and we plan on fighting vehemently to prove his innocence," his attorney said. He breathed a huge sigh of relief that LaRon hadn't exploded.

India hugged her brother once more before she left him in the hands of the sheriffs. She totally ignored all the reporters. As she drove away, she passed Clyde Dexter. He obviously got word her brother had just turned himself in. The two locked eyes. She drove straight to Jocelyn's house to fill her in on what was going on and to pick up her little sisters, who had spent the night there.

SEVEN

Dip was back at his house with his three-man crew. News of the sting operation had all their eyes transfixed on his 64" flat-screen TV mounted on the wall. The breaking news coverage came after Red and Joel both got calls from people telling them of police activity.

"And as the numbers continued to rise of those arrested across the city, we were told that the leader of this ring, LaRon Jones Sr., is moments away from turning himself in."

The four looked at each other. The twenty-two kilos of cocaine sat at their feet. They made no preparation beyond getting back to Dip's crib with the shit. Watching the coverage, even Dip wondered if that was a good idea.

"Can this nigga be trusted?" A.D. asked. He had heard of the nigga, had seen him out clubbing a few times, but had no personal dealings with him.

Given his previous dealings with LaRon, if Dip had to give an answer, he'd say yes. But he heard some of the charges facing the nigga. Motherfuckers told for less. Hearing all them numbers and realizing that you might not get out of prison for the rest of your life broke most niggas, even those as thorough as LaRon. His thoughts were interrupted as LaRon pulled up on his bike and hugged his sister.

"Fuck!" A.D. exclaimed loudly, causing everyone to look at him. He scooted up to the edge of his seat, staring at the TV. "Who the fuck is he hugging?"

"Oh," Dip smiled. Yeah, India was the real deal. Beautiful wasn't enough to describe her looks. "That's his sister, India. Don't waste your time, nigga. She's outta your league."

"Nigga must not know. Ain't no bitch outta my league—white, black, rich, poor. They all can be had by this nigga," A.D. boasted.

Dip let him have his dream. He had no idea who India was waiting on. For some time he thought she had to be gay, but he soon realized that wasn't her thing either. Her knight in shining armor wasn't sitting across from him. That much he knew. But Dip was beginning to like the young nigga A.D. He reminded him of himself when he was young and single.

"The nigga turns out to be a rat, I'm spanking him," Joel proclaimed.

"Nigga, you always want to kill some motherfuckin' body," Red told the hot-tempered youngster.

"I'm just saying, the nigga knew what it was hittin' for when he got in the game. Don't bitch up now 'cuz you busted. It's all a part of it."

"Told you the nigga's name should be Angry Smurf. Nigga always mad at some shit," A.D. teased his childhood friend. He scrunched up his face and balled up his hands. "I hate snitches. I hate bitches. Nigga, I hate, hate, hate!"

Dip, Red, and A.D. all laughed.

"I got your hate, bitch-ass nigga," Joel said, never even cracking a smile as he tapped the nine he had on the table. He was the only nigga with his shit out. Wouldn't catch him slippin' ever. If you did, kill him, is how he saw it.

They finished watching the news coverage. Dip made the decision for them. "Until we find out what's going on, we got to lay low." He left out when they did with the twenty-two kilos in his trunk. Never in his life had he been so nervous. He kept his eyes in the rearview and side mirrors trying to spot a tail. There was none. He made it safely to the storage area on the South side right off of Carson Street. Later on, he'd buy some furniture and move it into storage, along with the twenty-two keys.

A.D. was quick linking up with Red when the nigga outlined the plan to him. He was getting it, but not on the level that he wanted. His pockets weren't empty, but they weren't full either. The shit Red laid down and seeing the twenty-two birds had his head spinning. The most he'd seen at one time was one bird.

"Where you headed, nigga?" Joel asked. He had his own ride, but was still feeling it from a late night out of drinking. On some real shit, he wanted to go back to sleep. He had the seat leaned all the way back and his eyes were closed.

"Shorty from the club last night hit me up. Told her I was swinging past for a meal."

Joel was about to tell the nigga he was always chasing some pussy, but the mention of a meal stopped him. He realized he hadn't eaten since nine the previous night. "Bitch better know how to cook."

"Who said she cookin' for you, nigga?"

"My feet, nigga. When you stop this car and get out, my ass is following you."

A.D. laughed. It was just like it had always been since Joel moved into his Westside neighborhood. The niggas were each other's shadow. He thought about the time they met . . .

Tony (a.k.a. Anthony David, a.k.a. A.D.), age nine, looked on as everyone else did as the U-Haul truck came to a stop in front of the row house he also lived in. The only available house was the one right next to the one he lived in. Everyone was curious to see who was about to move in. The people that moved out hadn't been gone a week and now someone was already moving in. The truck stopped.

Standing in the court besides Tony and several other youngsters were a group of teenagers smoking a blunt.

"Welcome to Paradise," one of the boys said as a black man and white woman got out of the truck. When he opened up the back, four young kids jumped down. "Man, they fuckin' half breeds," Tony pointed out as everyone started to laugh.

The tallest of the children, although he was small for his age, ran before his parents could stop him and tackled the boy that called him a half breed.

Tony hadn't been prepared for the attack. It caught him off guard. He could fight and had quite a rep for himself, but this little nigga was strong and quick, despite his pudgy frame.

"Yeah, nigga, talk that shit now," the boy said as he punched repeatedly.

Tony managed to break away and get to his feet. He shot a quick jab out that connected.

He was breathing heavily and felt blood trickling down his face.

The black man stopped his wife before she could stop their son. His son needed this fight. Oh, he'd whoop his ass later for fighting, but right now this would define their survival amongst the kids. Win or lose, the kids knew his son would fight.

Knowing that a fight was going on, a crowd soon gathered. People yelled directions to the youngsters and ooooh and aaahed when a punch was connected.

It was a woman who came out and grabbed the slim brown-skinned boy by his torn shirt, which prompted the man to grab his own son. She smacked the boy she held. "Out here fighting in your good clothes. Get your ass in the house." She shoved the boy in front of her.

Flex looked down at his son. He would have a black eye and he had blood coming out of his busted lip, but he was okay. He decided he wouldn't beat him. He handed him the door key and smiled at him. "Go clean yourself up."

They would fight once more, but after that, the two would be best friends. What they could never agree upon is who won the fights.

Joel and A.D. finally made it to the girl's house. Her name was Taylor, and she was from and lived in Homewood on Monticello Street. She was light skinned, with long hair and an onion-shaped ass. Her hair was pulled back now. The good thing was she looked just as good in the daytime as she did the night before.

Even her crib was an improvement from what he usually got from joints he met in the club.

Some of them were apologizing at the door for

the condition of their home. Others blamed their junky homes on their kids. This house was clean and so far no children came running out asking for money.

Taylor was surprised that he had his boy with him. He didn't say anything about bringing someone. It was cool though. "Y'all can sit down in the living room. Either of y'all want something to drink?"

"What you got?" Joel asked.

She giggled. "Pretty much whatever you want besides Patron," she said, recalling his drink of choice from the night before.

Just the mention of alcohol turned his stomach. "Cold water is cool."

"Whose sticks?" A.D. asked, picking up the controller to the PlayStation 2. "You got kids?"

"Hell no! I just turned twenty-one, and whose house is it? The Station is mine!"

A.D. didn't tell her that he just smashed a twenty-one-year-old shorty from the west that had four kids and none of them was twins. Real talk. He didn't think the siblings had the same dad.

Four kids and four baby dads. That scenario wasn't uncommon. What was uncommon was that Taylor at twenty-one had none and had her own spot. "You got Madden?"

She returned with two bottled waters. "Yeah,

beside the TV's the games."

The flat screen sat on a glass table. It had to be a 42" TV. A.D. was impressed. "Your last nigga hustled or something?"

Taylor smacked her lips. "The last nigga I fucked with was far from a hustler. I got a job and I go to school. Everything you see in this crib I paid for. What type of women are you used to dealing with?"

Again, he wasn't going to comment on that. He didn't want to fuck up his chances with her. Shorty was a keeper.

"You want some work?" she asked as she picked up the wireless remote.

"For real?" If she knew how to play Madden, he was wifing her.

"I'm the burgh, nigga."

Joel looked at them, mad as a motherfucker. He was hungry. "Nigga, give me the keys. I'm going to Mickey D's."

A.D. handed him the keys to his car. "Grab me a number one."

The nigga had to have lost his mind. He snatched up the keys and left out. "Eat Madden, nigga."

The two, who were already into the football game, barely noticed his departure. It was the start of something new.

EIGHT

LaRon was taken to the county jail on 2nd Avenue by the sheriff he was turned over to. With the handcuffs on his wrist and shackles on his ankles, he sat in the back of the sheriff's car staring at the people and streets, wondering when he'd be a free man again.

"Sheriff's bringing in one newbie," the driver said when the voice came over the small intercom right next to the secured gate.

It reminded LaRon of the drive-thru at McDonald's. But no voice said, "Welcome to McDonald's. May I take your order."

The gate began to slide, allowing the car he was riding in to pass through. They drove a short distance to another gate. No intercom was there. High up on the wall was a camera. The gate began to open.

LaRon smiled as the car began to move. He didn't find shit funny. He just thought of the movie *SWAT* when the nigga yelled into the camera, "I'll give anyone that breaks me out of jail $100 million." He had $10 million. The gate began to lower. He'd never been in jail before. He knew shit was about to get real.

The sheriff and the deputy got out of the car and went to a group of steel. Mom boxes. They both took off their guns and put them in a box. "No Guns Beyond This Point" signs were on the wall. Damn, his strap wasn't on his hip, and he felt naked. The door opened and he swung his leg out, causing the shackle to bite into the flesh of his ankle.

"Take your time," the sheriff told him.

He did. Yet even walking slow the steel still bit into his skin. The sheriff opened the door for him.

"Face the wall."

LaRon did as he was told. He really wasn't in a position not to do as he was told. A door to his right buzzed and three correctional officers came in.

The room was about seven by fourteen feet wide and long. Really not big enough to hold the six people standing in it.

"I'll go handle the paperwork," the deputy said. The sheriff grabbed hold of the cuffs. "Stay facing the wall until both sets of cuffs are off," he instructed.

Again, he followed directions.

"Lift your right foot. Now your left." The shackles were off. He wanted to rub his ankles, but more orders were given, this time by one of the guards.

"Put your feet in the prints and empty out everything in your pockets and place the items on the bench."

He listened to the guard give each command and wondered how many times he said each one and whether he said them in his sleep. "Lift your right foot. Left foot. Run your hands across your hair. Turn your head to the left. Right. Open your mouth, etc." He began to sound like a robot to LaRon. Finally it was over. It was nothing like the movie *Oz* where you had to take off all your clothes and bend over and cough.

"Follow me."

LaRon did, after putting everything on the bench back in his pockets, minus his set of keys and pack of Newports. The ACJ was a non-smoking facility. He stepped out of the small room and put his back up against the wall. Immediately, he heard his name being called. Niggas locked up in cells stood pressed up against the glass. He recognized a few, but none were from his crew. He raised his hand in greeting.

"Thoughts of suicide."

His attention was brought back to the nurse standing in front of him. "Ever tried to kill yourself, or do you have any suicidal thoughts now?" This bitch was crazy.

"Hell no," he said instantly.

"Drug use—crack, heroin, PCP?"

He answered no to all her questions, and she moved away.

"LaRon."

He looked up and recognized the nigga motioning him with his finger. The nigga was from East Liberty or some shit.

"Big baller," the guard said. He didn't say "Never thought I'd see you here," because he knew who stood in front of him. This is where they all ended up one day or another.

LaRon stepped up to the counter and let the man put a band around his arm that he wrote his name on. He didn't know if this nigga was on some hating shit or what. He kept his expression neutral. He noticed how everyone, all the guards behind the counter and a few prisoners in white, were looking at him.

"Cops sent in word to keep you separated from all those others brought in, but I figure you might want to holla at them. They don't run shit in here," the guard said in a low tone to him as he put on the armband. "One for lockup."

"Which cell?" another guard asked as he walked up, pulling a set of keys out of his pocket.

"Big room," he instructed.

LaRon nodded at the black man behind the counter. Next time he saw him, he'd look out for the nigga. As soon as he stepped in the room he would be going in, niggas from his team jumped to their feet. The door opened and LaRon walked into an embrace with a smile on his face. This was sorta like a reunion. Some of the people he hugged, he was meeting for the first time.

Those that weren't a part of his crew looked on. Everyone began to talk at once, asking a million different questions.

"We can all sing together, my niggas, but we all can't talk together," LaRon told everyone. He motioned everyone to the furthest part of the cell, near the toilet-sink combo. The dudes that were already occupying that part of the room weren't dumb enough to sit there after LaRon motioned them to vacate.

"Listen to me," he whispered as he put his back up against the wall and the twenty or so people huddled around him. "These niggas are coming at us hard. Ain't no snitching. Everybody is going to have an attorney, and whoever can make bond will get out, word on my baby bro." He looked at each person, wanting to say more, but right now wasn't a time for words. Too many ears.

The stories started coming out on how they got nabbed. Even LaRon laughed at the tales. "Heard the niggas yell 'police,' but, niggas," one nigga said as he told his story, "this bitch's pussy wouldn't release me so I could grab my strap."

"What's her name?"

"Gina," the storyteller revealed. "From the East Short—light skin?"

"Yeah."

"Man, I smashed that too. Nigga ain't lying."

Everyone laughed. The stories kept going, and then the door opened. "LaRon Jones," the guard called out.

He pounded niggas as he walked out of the room.

"Detectives are here to see you," the guard told him.

He followed the man back up to the door that he came through. The two detectives stood waiting on him. "Is my attorney aware of this?"

"Mr. Jones, we are wondering if you'd like to talk to us."

"Ain't got shit to say to y'all."

Clyde figured as much. He'd gambled and lost. He'd request to talk to each one of those they arrested. Eventually he'd find someone who would be willing to talk. He always did.

LaRon watched as a woman was brought out of the back of a cop car. Fannie Oliver from the bank. She was in tears and didn't notice him. He wondered if Dip got everything out of the bank. For his sake and hers, he hoped he did. "When do I get to make a phone call?"

"As soon as you are processed."

The guard turned and led the way back to the cell. LaRon had to get her out. He wondered where her husband was.

On the outside, the hours went by slowly for India. She waited for news from her brother's attorney about her brother. She'd be at the preliminary hearing on 1st Avenue at the municipal courthouse. She was told that could take up to six hours. Why it would take so long, she couldn't figure.

"Is he going to get out?" Carla asked.

Both girls had cried when they got news of their brother's arrest. They were fearful that once again their family would be snatched away from them and they'd be on their own.

"Yes," India answered her sister. She hugged them. "No one is going to tear us apart."

"You promise?" Sandra asked softly.

"Promise." Whatever she had to do, India would make sure she kept her word.

Standing outside the courthouse waiting on her brother Balil and LaRon's lawyer, she watched the convoy of DAs and police officers begin to make their way into the courthouse. One of the men was Clyde Dexter. The two locked eyes for the third time that day. "I promise," she repeated.

There were several people called before LaRon's name was eventually called.

Although she never defended anyone in a real courtroom, she recognized several of the DAs that lined the halls. Several news anchors milled about. The long wait seemed to have drained everyone. Carla and Sandra begged India to let them stick around so they could see their brother. Those two were showing signs of being irritable. Despite India telling her to stay home, Deamber was there.

Families of others waiting for their locked-up family, men, and friends filled the halls. "This is the big fish," India heard the man she recognized as the head district attorney say. He headed in and she made her way right behind him. People who were already in made their way out.

"Commonwealth versus LaRon Jones Senior."

LaRon appeared, shuffling his way to the place where he was told to stand. He smiled when he saw his family.

Carla and Sandra both waved, and Deamber

began to cry lightly. Standing alongside of the head DA was Det. Clyde Dexter.

The long list of charges being read by the magistrate seemed to go on forever. It finally came to an end.

"Who is here representing the state?"

"I am, Your Honor. For the record, my name is Ivan Russell."

"Do you have any witnesses that you want to testify?"

"Yes, Your Honor. Detective Clyde Dexter."

He was sworn in and then the DA began his questions. His work history, his assignment on the case involving LaRon. Finally, it was over.

"Bail on this case is being denied at this time."

"Your Honor, my client has no arrest history. He has several businesses around the city. He turned himself in to the authorities. He's been a resident of Allegheny his entire life. He poses no risk of fleeing. He is not charged with capital murder."

"Because of the seriousness of the case, no bond is set. A bond hearing will be scheduled five days from today." The Judge ordered and pounded his gavel in conclusion.

Deamber made her way to the front where a gate separated her from LaRon. "I love you, baby."

"Love you too, lil mami."

"Where are they taking him? You said he was going to get out," Carla said.

India grabbed the hands of each of her sisters and made eye contact with her brother. No words were needed between the two.

After leaving the courthouse, he had to wait until everyone in the small room saw the magistrate. He didn't have a long wait. Once the handcuffs and shackles came off, he was led to a holding room that had eight phones and vending machines. He headed straight to the crowded phone.

"Baby, I'll call you right back," a dude that was a part of his team said. "Here you go, fam," he said to LaRon.

A dude stepped forward and reached for the phone. "I was waiting on this, partner."

LaRon was already mad as hell and was a split second from hitting the nigga. "And you still waiting, nigga," came the voice behind him.

LaRon turned and saw Ken Oliver, the husband of Fannie. Bunched up with him was a pack of niggas from his crew.

Seeing he was outnumbered, the nigga backed up.

"They got your wife," he told the man in case he didn't know.

"Yeah, it ain't about shit. One thing that bitch

can do is act. She'll have them motherfuckers apologizing before it's all over."

LaRon was listening while he was dialing his attorney's number. "Who got bonds?"

Some had bonds, but because of detainers, wasn't no sense in paying the bonds. Those that could post bond stepped up and handed LaRon their paperwork. "You got a pen?" he said into the phone. "Pull over nigga," he instructed. When his attorney told him he was ready, he gave him the seventeen names of the people whose paperwork he had in his hands. "Post their bonds now. The money will meet you there." After talking to his attorney a little more, he hung up. He pushed in his sister's number.

"Hey, Sis," he said with a smile.

Hearing her brother's voice put a smile on her face. "How are you holding up?"

"You act like I've been busted for years," he laughed.

"Yes, this is LaRon. Will you two just wait?"

He missed his baby sisters. "Let me talk to them."

"Being the oldest, he was my brother first, but he wants to talk to y'all," she joked with her impatient sisters.

He talked to both of them, and then India got back on the phone. He calculated how much he needed to pay for all seventeen bonds. Going through a bondsman, which he intended on doing, he would only have to pay a percentage of each bond—money that he wouldn't be getting back. It came to $18,750. He told his sister where to meet his attorney. They talked for fifteen minutes, then the phone hung up. He called Deamber and talked to her for the next hour. For awhile, the phone would be his best friend.

After he talked to Deamber, he used one more call to speak to a girl he'd been seeing off and on for the last year.

"Make sure you put me on your visiting list."

LaRon had no clue about visits or any of that shit. He'd tried to cut it off with one girl, but after she cried and professed to love him, he smashed on the living room floor. Missy was only eighteen years old and went by the name Jada. At least that's what everyone called her fine ass. She looked just like girly in the movie *Set It Off* with Queen Latifah and Vivica Fox. When she rocked her shades and sucked on a cherry lollipop, LaRon was gone. With him about to be a married man, he shouldn't be cheating, but he had a weakness for her fine ass.

"You trying to fire up something, nigga?"

He saw the person talking to him was one of his crew. What he really needed was a fuckin Newport.

He didn't realize he was addicted to cigarettes until they took his pack. He covered up the phone. "You got a square?" He saw the loose tobacco the young nigga flashed. "Call you back, babe." He hung up and one of his crew snatched up the phone. LaRon followed a few of his niggas into a cell. "How y'all get that shit in?"

"Nigga from upstate in that cell sold me a finger for fifty dollars."

LaRon watched him roll the tobacco up in a torn piece of toilet paper wrapper. He wasn't feeling smoking tobacco out of toilet paper, but he needed that nicotine. "Does the nigga have any more?"

"Probably. I'll holla at him," Marcus said. He knew the nigga from the streets.

"Buy it all." He pulled out his roll of money and counted out $500. He took the roll up and inhaled deeply. Despite the wrapping, it tasted just like a Port. Actually, better than a Newport.

Several others began to roll up, so LaRon finished that one off. He was cool after that.

He returned to the phone.

By the time he got his picture taken and had a plastic armband with his picture, his jail number 609687, and name on it placed on his right wrist, several of the crew were being released.

"Keep it a hundred out there, my niggas," he

instructed. "They probably are still gonna watch y'all, so lay low." He pulled Ken to the side. He was one of the ones that was leaving. "You know the nigga Dip from Saint Clair? Holla at him and tell him it's all good. Tell him my sis will get at him."

"I'll handle that," Ken told him. "You need me to handle anything else?"

LaRon wasn't sure how things would go, but he needed niggas out there that would put in work if it came to that. "Link up with Dip and be ready to move out."

Ken was in the game a lot longer than LaRon. He was forty-two years old and saw the change in the game. Some of these same niggas that he just bonded out would turn on him if given the chance. Ken was old school. He'd be there for the nigga when the snitching started. "I got you. Call me."

The two hugged, and LaRon watched him go through the door. "Lockup time. Find a cell," the female guard called out.

He saw niggas waiving him to a cell they had already locked down. There were no outsiders, so he'd have some time to talk to them.

By the time he saw the nurse and gave the guard his money, $9,400, he was tired as hell. His hip hurt from lying on that hard-ass steel bench. He had a crook in his neck from using a roll of toilet paper as a pillow. He heard from niggas that had been locked up before that the mattresses were so thin it felt like you were still sleeping on steel. He didn't give a fuck. He just wanted to lay down.

"LaRon Jones," the guard called out.

He had been called with a group of other prisoners to get showered so they could go upstairs. He stepped up to the counter. He was handed a red pair of pants, red shirt, and a towel.

"Follow me."

"Strip down and hand me your clothing one item at a time."

"What?"

"Is this your first time here? You know the routine."

He could tell the punk-ass white dude was being smart. "This is my first time here."

"Good for you. Do as I say and we'll get through this. Take your damn clothes off."

"Man, don't talk to me like that."

"Are you disobeying an order?"

Before LaRon could tell the bitch-ass nigga fuck his order, the curtain at the door was slid to the side.

"Is there a problem?"

The white rookie smiled. Blues stuck together. He hadn't had the chance to beat someone's ass yet, but he saw video footage of other guards getting into it with prisoners. He was ready for his beat down. "He refuses to strip."

"I'll handle this one," the muscled black man said.

The rookie wanted to be a part of the beat down, but he left. His time would come. LaRon wasn't a beefy dude, but he wasn't a bitch either. Lee Haney wannabe could get it too.

"My little brother told me you good people," the guard said when it was just the two of them. "His name is Tarue."

LaRon knew now why the guard looked familiar. Tarue was one of his niggas. He smiled. Tarue was one of the niggas he told to get rid of the work and burn the cribs. "The nigga cool."

He shrugged. "You know that nigga. He on bond for that other shit, so he took off." There were a few niggas on the run. Sitting in the jail now, he felt like he should've run.

"Good look people."

"Trying to push you through. Will get as many people from your crew up on 4-A."

"What's that?"

"One of our intake pods. Is there anyone specifically you want up there?"

He shook his head no. He wasn't too close with any of them. "Send as many as you can."

"I'll handle that. Go ahead and put your street clothes in that plastic bin and jump in the shower if you don't mind."

LaRon chose to skip the shower. He put on the red uniform and walked out. The wait wasn't that long to go upstairs. On 4-A, he went to the desk with the group he came up with and waited to be assigned a cell. He heard his name being called from people already locked in their cells. He looked up and several cell lights were blinking on and off. He heard niggas saying their names, but he really couldn't hear them and definitely couldn't see them. He snatched up a thin green mattress and walked up to cell 213.

"What's up?" the dude he'd share a cell with said.

The top bunk didn't have a mattress on it, so he put his mat up there. His celly was an older dude that LaRon could tell right off was a crackhead. His busted down sneakers sat under the bed and had the whole cell smelling like corn chips. He wasn't on no ignorant shit, so he spoke. "What's up?" He put the sheet on the mat and pulled out the tobacco he had bought. "You smoke, ole timer?"

"Like a motherfucker, young buck."

Nothing really sounded like it should because the nigga was missing most of his teeth and all his fronts he needed to pronounce shit correctly. He had to fight off the urge to laugh. He rolled up two knowing the nigga would wet the tip all up. "Here, old head." He smoked his solo and asked his celly if he needed the light.

"It stays on all night."

LaRon tried to flick it off to no avail. He jumped up in the bed, rolled up the extra set of reds, covered up with the blanket and was asleep within ten minutes.

It was 1:45 a.m. when he got to sleep, ending his first, but not last, day in jail.

NINE

Jocelyn was in her office in the rec center when
Denean came and told her the police wanted to
talk to her. Despite her past crack addiction, she'd
never been arrested. They ran into a house one time
that she was getting high in, but she didn't have
anything on her, and after running her name, they
let her go. Still, having the police asking to see her
made her nervous.

She had no idea what they wanted to see her
about.

Michelle, a friend of hers, who worked at the
center, gave her a worried look. Michelle had lost
her child, a fifteen-year-old daughter named Kelly,
after someone ran into her home trying to steal
Jocelyn's son's drugs that he kept stashed there. The
two shared a close friendship and shared their loss
of their children to violence, to audiences around the
city.

"May I help you?" Jocelyn asked the two men
that stood by the door.

"Ms. Wright, I'm Agent Duffy and that's Agent
Walter. We're FBI agents and we have a court order

to gather all the paperwork on this facility."

"What? Wait. What does this have to do with?"

"Ma'am, we are here under court order. You are welcome to review the order." He held out the papers he had in his hand.

She took them, but had no clue what she was looking at. "Excuse me, I have to make a phone call." She stepped away and called India. "The FBI are here with a court order . . . Okay." She returned to the agents. "Sir, my attorney is on the way. You can start your search, but until my attorney gets here, I am not answering any questions."

That the feds were at the recreational center was a bad sign for her brother. She figured that eventually the feds would pick up his case. She'd talked to him just that morning and there was no mention of the feds contacting him. When she talked to his attorney, the man said he expected this. Now they both were headed for the rec center. With the feds involved, she knew they'd leave no rock unturned and no bridge uncrossed. She'd have to move the money soon. The window of opportunity was closing.

Hercules Reynolds went over the order, seeing nothing he could dispute. He had Jocelyn send all the kids and employees home. He remained with Jocelyn, India, and Denean as the twenty plus agents collected their evidence. Some of the money that funded the rec had come from LaRon, but he'd used money from other legal ventures for it. His name was on the books, but he conducted no illegal activities there. For the most part, Hercules saw this move as a gathering of evidence—a fact-finding mission as they built the case on LaRon and his crew.

The two different legal agencies went about things differently. The feds were much more thorough and searched deeper for evidence. And that's what had Hercules worried. He was LaRon's personal attorney, but he also helped him clean his dirty money. Several stocks LaRon had, Hercules, with the help of his wife, started. There were properties in his name that he turned over to a real estate company owned by LaRon.

As the agents began to pack up computers they confiscated and file cabinets, Hercules breathed a huge sigh of relief. And then his world came crashing down.

"Hercules Reynolds , I am a federal marshal here to serve you a summons to appear in front of a grand jury."

The man's voice became blurred, and for the first time in his life, the kid that went by the name "Motor Mouth" had nothing to say. And then his fate was sealed. "Your wife is also summoned to appear."

His dear, sweet wife. He couldn't allow that to happen.

India watched the attorney break out in a cold sweat. She knew the man wasn't built for a jail cell, and she knew he'd turn on her brother. She'd have to convince him not to turn into a snitch. "If your job is done here, I'm asking that you men please leave so we can straighten up the mess."

After several minutes, all the feds were gone, and Hercules broke down sobbing. "What am I going to do? I'm ruined. I can't go to jail. I just can't."

India wanted to slap the nearly hysterical man and tell him to pull it together. Like everyone else involved, things were fine when LaRon paid them nicely. Now when the flip side of the game hit them, they couldn't take it. "Pull yourself together." Her cell phone rang and she saw it was Mike Astari. "Hello."

"India, trouble. Rats in your brother's organization."

She listened as he told her about the three men trying to work out a deal with the cops. "The feds are picking up the case," she revealed.

"I can silence these canaries for you."

India smiled despite the seriousness of the situation. "Thank you, Mike, but I can handle this. Just have the oven heated up for me."

He knew what that meant. India was a deadly woman.

"Jocelyn and Denean, go home. I'll lock up. Hercules, we have to talk."

TEN

A.D. couldn't believe he let her convince him to go to Sandcastle with her. He stood waiting on her to come out of the locker room, unable to take his eyes off the women that passed by him. He said "damn" so many times in the span of ten minutes, that you would have thought that was each woman's name. He made eye contact with a big-butt cute-ass white girl, unable to believe the dimension of her ass. Kim Kardashian didn't have shit on shorty.

"Dumb-ass nigga. Who brings a bitch to Sandcastle?" Joel asked, even though the girl Taylor hooked him up with was right. He told hooked-ass A.D. that the Castle wasn't the place to go. "Too many bad bitches there."

This time A.D. agreed with his boy. He had to holla at white girly as soon as he got the chance. He didn't usually play in the snow, but . . .

"Damn," came the word spoken by a female. She was so close to him that A.D. turned and smiled, thinking she was talking to him. Then he saw she wasn't even looking at him. He saw what evoked the word out of her, and his mouth opened in shock.

Walking toward him in her two-piece swimsuit, a sarong across her hips, and her shades on was Taylor. Her eyes locked on him as she made her way slowly toward him. He couldn't think of a word to describe the shit, but angelic. Her beauty was unreal, out of this world. The way people parted and stared at her, you'd have thought she had dropped out of the sky. Even the sun seemed to shine on her brighter than those around her.

"Hey, babe," she said, kissing him on the lips. He had finally kissed her, but she still hadn't slept with him.

"Excuse me, sexy. I ain't gay, but you are gorgeous," the woman who said "damn" said.

Taylor smiled, and that made her even more beautiful. "Thank you, and so are you. And I ain't gay either." The two laughed before the woman left. Taylor linked arms with A.D. "Come on, baby."

He knew he was the envy of every nigga at the pool. And he didn't feel weird about her holding onto his arm, even though it was an act, like handholding, he considered too white. It felt good to him. In fact, he pulled her closer.

He thought Taylor would be on some cute shit, but she got on the slides without hesitation, not bothering to wear a cap. He'd come with no real intent of getting in the water. In fact, he still had his money in his pocket when Taylor managed to push both of them into the water. Even Joel laughed as he was caught off guard. Being around her put everyone in a good mood.

"She's good people," Joel revealed as they went to get something to snack on.

"What? Nigga, you like somebody other than me?"

"Nigga, don't act like I am on some down-low shit. I'm just saying she ain't like the hood rats you used to dealing with."

A.D. had to agree. He turned to look in her direction and he saw some niggas standing near her. For the first time in his life, he got jealous. He wouldn't admit that to anyone, but he knew the rage at seeing niggas standing over her was jealousy.

Joel saw his boy's expression change, and he turned and looked in the direction of where they had left the girls. "What's wrong, homie?"

The dudes walked off. "Nothin', fam."

"Nigga, you got the best thing walking out this motherfucker today. Niggas gonna try to holla. Don't trip."

Joel wasn't usually the voice of reason. He was the one wanting to set it off, the one that had to be calmed down, not the one trying to calm him down. A.D. grabbed up the nachos and soda. "I'm cool, my nigga."

The two friends headed back toward the girls. A.D. knew it was about to be trouble when the four dudes then surrounded Taylor and Sasha. He hurried over to them.

"I'm cool," he heard Taylor say. She still hadn't seen A.D. approaching. She was sitting up now.

"Let me get that number, lil mami .And let a nigga like me show you another side of life."

"I'm taken, honestly, but thank you."

"Man, fuck that bitch, cuz. She ain't all that," one of the men said.

"For real though, I got to be a bitch 'cuz I'm taken. That's fucked up," she said as she was getting to her feet. And then she saw him.

A.D.'s anger went into overdrive when the nigga called Taylor a bitch. He dropped the food and soda in the grass and prepared to take on the four of them. Taylor was quick to wrap her arms around him.

"Baby, they ain't worth it," she said as she held him tightly.

One of the four men laughed: the one trying to get her number. "Yeah, nigga, listen to your bitch. It ain't worth dying over no pussy."

A.D. broke loose from her hold, but Joel grabbed him. "Cool out, fam. The niggas' got heat."

Then A.D. saw the guns tucked in their swim trunks, their T-shirts covering them.

"Just what I thought. Fake ass nu-nu. You ever want to get with a G, holla at me." He recited his number and then they turned and walked away.

Taylor turned A.D.'s face and kissed him on the lips. "Them niggas just hatin', baby."

Yeah, they were, but that still didn't change the fact A.D. had just gotten punked.

Joel was furious that the niggas had come at his and his boy's neck like that. If his strap hadn't been in the car, they would've had a shootout right there next to the pool. "Let's get the fuck outta here, fam. I'm feelin' naked."

A.D. felt the same way. "Grab your shit. We outta here."

Taylor collected her things, along with her girl Sasha. She didn't know why people couldn't go out and have a good time without finding trouble or trouble finding them.

Sasha, more into the street life than her friend, knew this was far from over. She grabbed her friend's hand.

Outside in the parking lot, A.D. instructed Taylor to take his truck and go wait for him at the gas station. She didn't want to split up with him, but Sasha pulled her along.

They only had to wait a little more than an hour before the four niggas came out laughing. They didn't notice the car coming toward them with the window down and the muzzle of the AK sticking out. One of the girls they were flirting with screamed as she noticed the gun and the bandana-faced gunman. Joel pulled the trigger. Bodies fell as bullets ripped into them. He wanted to empty the whole clip, but A.D. pulled out.

At the gas station, Joel took the license plate he had just stolen off of the car that was parked next to his, and replaced it with his old one.

Taylor watched them in silence. She waited on A.D. nervously. Sasha got out of A.D.'s truck and got in Joel's car, while Taylor and A.D. got in A.D.'s truck.

"You hungry, sexy?" A.D. asked Taylor as he started up the truck.

* * *

Dip knew who Ken was. What he didn't know is the woman who worked in the bank was his wife. When he got the call from Ken saying they had to meet, he was slightly hesitant. He knew Ken from his days of hustling, but anyone that LaRon dealt with was suspect right then. Still, when Ken said he had a message from LaRon, Dip had to hear it.

The two met downtown at Point State Park at the water fountain. Dip watched him approach, taking care to scan the crowd of people. It wasn't that he could spot an undercover, but he felt good just looking around.

"What's good, Dip? It's been a long time." Ken didn't even know Dip was back in the game. The two hugged.

"Trying to make it, that's all," Dip responded. "How is LaRon holding up?"

Ken took out a pack of cigarettes and fired one up. He started walking. "You know the young nigga is a soldier. He got old-school blood running through his veins. Not artificial Kool-Aid these Similac babies got coursing through theirs."

"I feel that."

"You got that shit out just in time people. Soon after you left, they ran in there and snatched my wife up."

Dip nodded, not really wanting to commit to anything. Short of patting the nigga down, he didn't know if Ken could be trusted. "What did LaRon say?"

"His sis would be getting at you, but that it's cool to unload that."

That was music to Dip's ears. "Tell him I'll

handle that."

"Bet." Ken shook Dip's hand and bounced. It was his time to get his shit in order. His wife was out, but they still were facing charges and he had no idea that they would soon be re-arrested under a federal indictment.

Dip got on his phone on the way back to his car and called Red. "It's all good, fam. Just got word from LaRon."

"Was just about to hit you up with some better news than that," Red revealed.

Dip couldn't figure what news that could be. They had twenty-two birds in their possession that they could start to get rid of. There was nothing better than that.

"I got the niggas that ran up in your shit."

Maybe there was. "Where you at?" He got the location and headed there. Knowing that in a little while the niggas responsible for putting a gun to his wife's and children's heads would soon be dead he felt on top of the World. He was all the way back in.

* * *

The warehouse was abandoned. It was located on Butler Street in Lawrenceville. Dip drove around the back as Red instructed him to. It was just turning dark as the sun began to set. He parked and got out. Red's car, A.D.'s truck, and a car he didn't recognize were parked as well. He stepped between the broken panel.

Three dudes were tied up and lying on the dirt floor. Even with the beating John had taken and a rag stuffed in his mouth, Dip still recognized the guy as his neighbor. The laid-back family man that worked his nine to five faithfully couldn't be one of the ones involved in the robbery. The other two, he had no clue who they were.

"Nigga was running his mouth and it got back to me, fam."

Dip knew eventually the niggas who got him would run their mouths or start spending. What he didn't expect is they'd get caught so soon. "Which one of you niggas put a gun to my kid's head?" It wasn't his neighbor because he knew the man's voice. He pulled the rag out of John's mouth. "Talk, nigga, and you better say the right shit."

John thought getting Roger would be an easy lick. He had no idea he was so entrenched in the streets. Now he knew he had fucked up and his life hung in limbo. "I got a safe in my house. Combo is 21-15-38."

Dip shot him in his leg. John screamed. "Wrong answer."

"Tay put the gun to your kid's head," he managed to get out.

"Which one of you niggas is Tay?" He looked at John, who turned his head and looked over at his two boys.

"The one at the end."

Dip walked and stood over the nigga that he couldn't wait to get his hands on.

Wordlessly, he shot the nigga in his kneecap. Then in his other leg. No one spoke as Tay screamed and passed out. "Where you got my money, nigga?" he asked the man in the middle.

The man knew his life was over, and he wasn't about to beg for his life. "Fuck your money, nigga, and fuck—"

He didn't get "you" out as Dip shot him in his mouth, killing him instantly.

John began to cry and beg for his life.

"Nigga, I want you to take this with you. Every time you used to kiss your wife goodbye and head to work, I used to creep over and let the bitch swallow my cum." He laughed loudly and shot John in his chest repeatedly. His body jumped as each round entered his body.

Tay moaned as he began to regain consciousness.

Dip pointed his gun at him and pulled the

trigger. It clicked empty. "Fuck."

"Don't trip, people," Joel said. "I got you." He put three into Tay's head.

Other than blood splatters on his pant leg and shoes, there was no sign that he had just participated in a triple homicide.

"Let's get out of here," Red said. He shot at niggas and got shot at before, but he never watched niggas get executed before. It was a little unnerving.

Everyone headed to the sports bar on Smallman in the strip. "We 'bout to start moving that weight," Dip informed them.

ELEVEN

LaRon woke up the next morning to the loud voice of a woman. "Come on, guys. It's breakfast time," she said over the loudspeaker.

It felt like he had just closed his eyes. They took his watch, so he couldn't even see what time it was. He rubbed his burning eyes.

"You eatin', young buck?"

He forgot all about having a celly. Old dude was already dressed, a cup and spoon in his hand, with the cell door open.

"Yeah," he answered. He sat up, his hip hurting worse than before.

"What's good, my nigga?"

The jump down to the floor wasn't as bad as he thought it would be. Several people were at his door, including two dudes in white. He stepped into his shoes.

"Uh-uh, y'all can come find a seat," the voice came over the intercom by the door. "Ain't no meeting being held."

"See you at the table."

"Word." He looked at the toothbrush and small-ass tube of toothpaste and made it do what it do. It left a nasty taste in his mouth.

"Last call for breakfast," came the annoying voice.

Damn. He wished she'd shut the fuck up. It was too early for the loud shit. He stepped out on the tier and looked down at everyone already seated at the tables. He saw some of his crew waving him over to a table they already had locked down. The guard was an old black woman with gray and black hair. She sat behind the desk writing something down. He sat down after giving several people a pound.

"First row," the guard called out.

"Where you get something to eat with?"

"Pantry, nigga, fam."

One of the dudes in the white—there were only four in white—brought him a cup and spoon. "What's up, LaRon? Saw your shit all on the news."

LaRon smiled. "Damn, nigga, how long you got in this bitch, life?"

"Two years, running wild. Four more months and it's over."

The dude he was speaking to was a nigga from Wilkinsburg that he knew.

"What's up with the white?"

"Worker nigga."

LaRon laughed. "Nigga, you ain't work on the street." Their table number was called and he got up with everyone else.

"Got you on another tray."

He got his tray and looked at the eggs, potatoes, a biscuit, and cornflakes. "Ain't no sugar."

"Under the biscuit," someone behind him said.

He moved the biscuit and saw the one packet of sugar. "I got biscuit for cereal."

"I got eggs for cereal."

"Potatoes and eggs for cereal."

Different people yelled out shit they wanted to trade across the room. LaRon didn't want any of the shit.

"Here, my nigga," he said, and set the tray on the table. He was hungry, but he wasn't that hungry yet to eat that shit.

"Come to my cell, fam. I got a bun for you," the worker said.

He followed him as people continued to trade shit. The bun he was handed was a monster honey bun. He fucked with them on the streets.

"Don't drink that chicory, fam."

"What's that?"

"Some nasty shit that's supposed to be coffee. I got you."

LaRon handed him the cup he reached for. He

returned with the cup full. "She be bringing in that Maxwell House."

He sipped the hot coffee and then opened up the bun with his teeth. The combination of the coffee and bun tasted better than a full-course meal.

"You trying to smoke something?" he offered.

"Definitely."

He already had something rolled from the night before. "Where you gonna do this at?"

"Y'all gotta lock up after chow. At around nine she gonna let y'all out. We can go to the gym."

The two stood there talking until it was time to take it back in their cells.

"LaRon, baby. You come on down and watch TV," the guard said over his intercom.

LaRon had no clue what that was about, but he was glad to be out of the cell. "Thanks," he said as he sat down. He had never watched *Good Morning America* in his life, but he watched it that morning.

"Shit is gravy," he informed his sister. "Tell Deamber to call that 1-800 number now and set up collect calls." He tried to call his woman on the house and her cell phone with no luck.

Since his home phone was through Comcast and her cell phone was through T-Mobile, collect calls would have to be prepaid.

India was happy to hear form her brother. She

knew they couldn't say too much over the phones, because they were recorded. It would have to wait. "You put in your visiting list?"

"A few minutes ago. The guard is going to handle that. Next visit is Wednesday. Y'all got to sign up an hour ahead of time." He talked to his little sisters before he hung up. He missed his woman and kids.

He went in the gym that had a backboard but no rim or ball, and blazed up. They walked in circles talking and joking.

Public defender investigators came onto the block. One called his name, but he told the cute white woman he had private counsel.

"LaRon, you got to go to Intake," the guard informed him.

He had no clue what that was about. He let a nigga from his crew hold his tobacco and lighter and left off the block.

"Where you going?" a guard asked.

"Intake."

"Stand by the elevators. Control, can I have 2 on 4 going to Intake."

"Fuck," a heavyset guard said as he got to his feet. "Wish they'd sent them all at one time."

The elevator came. They stepped on and rode it down to the ground. He saw a few people he knew and nodded at them in passing.

"LaRon Jones?" the guard behind the desk asked.

"Yeah?"

He pointed at two men in suits. "Here is your man."

"Mr. Jones, I'm Agent Marcus of the FBI. You are ordered to appear in front of the judge at the federal courthouse."

LaRon had no clue what any of this meant, but he wasn't dumb enough to speak. He allowed the man to pat him down and handcuff and shackle him.

"Would offer you a cigarette, but I see or rather smell that you have your own."

He guessed the motherfucker smelled the shit on him. He said nothing. Where the fuck was his attorney? He had no idea Attorney Reynolds had just been served his own set of papers.

The joinder case brought against LaRon charged him under the RICO Act as the leader of a mass cocaine ring tied to the Colombian Cartel. It was more extensive than the case brought against him by the state and revealed two things that scared the hell out of him: his attorney was indicted and there was the mention of informants.

* * *

While still at the rec center, India listened in on the call Hercules received from the attorney general. The call completely shook the man. She listened intently to his every word until he hung up.

"I'm ruined!" he exclaimed. Sweat and tears mingled as one. "I can't go to jail."

If running was an option, India would have sent him on his way. It wasn't. Eventually the man would get homesick or slip up and get caught, and they'd be right back where they started from. Sad to say, he had to go. "When do you have to see the AG?"

"As soon as everyone already locked up is charged. I figure a few days. Next week at the latest."

"That gives us some time." Actually, she meant it gave her some time.

"I can't sit in front of a grand jury."

She was thinking the exact same thing. There was no way he could be trusted to sit in front of a grand jury. And for that reason, he had to go.

"Go home to your family. I'll hire my brother a new attorney and also get you one. Don't worry about anything."

She locked up the recreational center and

walked the dejected attorney to his car. "We'll get through this."

He simply nodded his head, not feeling as confident. After he drove off, she called her brother Balil, who was watching their little sisters. She needed him. She also called Jocelyn and told her she needed her help and the help of her fiancé George. "It involves heavy lifting," she informed her.

"If I can lift it, I can help."

* * *

India entered the combination and swung the huge door open. George and Jocelyn stood in open-mouth amazement at the piles of money. Neither could believe their eyes.

"My brother's stash."

George had been in the game. Had a stash before, but nothing remotely close to what he was looking at now. He couldn't help it. "How much is there?"

"Eight to twelve million I guess," Balil said. "He stopped counting at seven mill."

"Do we got enough time to move it?"

India surely hoped so. By the time the feds focused on Hercules Reynolds, she planned to have all the money gone and the attorney disposed of.

To put all the money in duffel bags and move all

of it to the eighteen wheeler truck was an all-day affair. She wished her brother would have converted all the money into one hundred dollar bills before stashing it.

When they were almost finished, her cell phone rang. Drenched in sweat and tired, she took the time to sit on the edge of the couch.

"Are you watching the news?"

"The news? Why?"

"Turn on channel 14," Mike said.

She picked up the remote and turned on the TV, turning on the news.

"Again, in what appears to be a self-inflicted gunshot wound to the head, lawyer Hercules Reynolds has committed suicide," the news anchor said. "Facing a federal indictment in his connection with recently indicted LaRon Jones Senior, Attorney Reynolds was found in his study, by his wife. There will be more on this story at six."

She clicked off the TV. She was relieved in one aspect. His blood wouldn't be on her hands. But in the same sense, she wondered if he left a suicide note, and if he did, if it implicated her brother in any way. She hung up with the mobster.

"Let's hurry," she told the others. His death would bring the hounds in force.

TWELVE

Dip rented a home in Forest Hills. If he wasn't an established home owner and business man with a valid driver's license, he would have never moved out of the dangerous area to live. Ardmore Boulevard was as notorious as the stretch in Edgewood and Rankin. Sting operations went down regularly on the Boulevard. Besides that known fact, it wasn't that bad a spot to live in. The woman and her two children that he had moved in with made it appear that a well-grounded family was moving in.

The woman was a friend of Dip's—someone he knew and could trust. She was a secretary in a doctor's office in Oakland and the mother of two young children ages eleven and fourteen. The oldest was Dip's daughter—a known fact he himself didn't know until five years ago. The woman was the one woman he cheated with before his marriage. Not that it happened any time recently. He knew his wife wouldn't be happy with the situation. This wasn't a long-time situation though. He just wanted it to appear that a family was moving into the home. In two to three weeks, he planned on being the only one there. It would be a place to stash and cook up his coke. It was away from the inner city.

The alarm system he had installed was top-of-the-line, but the construction team he hired built him a nice safe that couldn't be detected. With the money he got out of Ken's safe (close to $600,000), he had enough to pay LaRon and still handle a few other things. It wasn't all his money, but he wasn't too worried about the rest.

Donna and the kids weren't there when he entered the house. He figured she had gone to Walmart to go food shopping. He told her they had to make it appear they were living there.

Most nights he wouldn't stay there, but his wife knew he was back in the game. Sometimes he'd tell her he was pulling an all-nighter, and she'd have no problem with it. He called India. "I got your brother's number," he told her.

"Good. He's been waiting on you to write him."

"Tell him it'll be in the mail today."

"Sounds good."

They hung up. Dip felt good. Once he handed India LaRon's money, he'd meet up with Red and then the nigga Andre from the North side. He'd finally be meeting the nigga that would handle the North side distribution.

* * *

Taylor wanted to tell him to stop, but it just felt too damn good. A.D. kissed her lightly several times on the nape of her neck. In the eight months since she'd been celibate, she hadn't been this weak for anyone. Until she found a man worthy of her, she planned on refraining from sex. From fifteen to seventeen, she wouldn't have classified herself as a hoe, but she engaged in sex when she wanted it. Twice even after she'd known the dude for only a few hours. In A.D., she saw something different, something lasting. Besides being attracted to one another, they had fun together, often laughing until their stomachs hurt. Giving herself to him seemed like the most natural thing to do.

He stood between her legs, pressed up against her phat ass, trying to control his breathing. Just the scent of her sent him over the edge. He knew her stance on sex and he respected it. Keeping it a hundred, not getting none had him fiending for it. Since he was twelve, he had never had to go more than two days after meeting someone before he hit it. It had been nearly a month since he met Taylor. He called himself a lame several times before he backed up.

Not having him pressed up on her had her sigh.

"What's wrong?"

He managed to only smile shyly. He couldn't tell her that if he continued to taste her sweetness, he'd end up tearing her clothes off.

Taylor turned to face him. Her fingers made a trail from his hairline to his jaw line. She kissed him tenderly as she grabbed the bottom of his shirt and pulled it over his head.

He trembled as her nails glided across his chest. When she bent, teased his nipples with her tongue, he had to stop her. "If you ain't ready, you better stop playing."

The smile she gave him was enough, but then she undressed slowly right before his eyes.

Completely naked she looked better than any woman he had ever had.

He lifted her up and carried her into her bedroom. "I love your sexy ass," he whispered to her.

Love, the thing she never had. "Make love to me, baby."

He did. And for both of them, it wasn't just sex, it wasn't fucking. They made love.

* * *

"Fuck me. Oh shit," Sasha screamed.

"That's right, papi, tear that pussy up," the Puerto Rican girl encouraged.

Joel continued to pound into Sasha as he hit it doggy style. The Rican girl was under him licking on his balls. When Sasha told him that she went both ways, he told her to hook some shit up. The girl that licked on his balls was not only a freak, but a dime. He was already on his third nut. Each time cumming up in Sasha. The three had been going at it for two hours when the Rican pulled his dick out and began to suck it. He leaned down and began to eat Sasha's pussy.

"Fuck me, papi," the Rican said. She lay on her back and pulled him on top of her.

The combination of the Goose, the X pills, and the Viagra he had taken had Joel on some other shit. Even after busting two nuts, he was still feeling strong. He mounted her and rammed into her, causing her to start speaking Spanish. The talk and her movement was too much. He nutted as his whole body shook.

That night three babies would be born—two to Joel and one to A.D. Each child would be their first. Actually, Joel's first and second.

THIRTEEN

Carla sat alone in the room she shared with her sister. Since leaving Philadelphia and coming to stay with her siblings, her whole life had changed—for the better. She loved the school she was attending, Kappa in the center of downtown. Sandra went to a special school in Oakland—a gifted school after it was revealed that she was a geek for real, a computer whiz. Carla always knew her sister was smart, but not that smart. Nonetheless, she was happy. And then her brother got arrested. Everything seemed to change. She never saw her sister. They never went anywhere anymore. Since he got arrested, she hadn't spent one night in her bed.

That they were finally home was short-lived. India told her to pack some clothes that they were going to spend a few nights over at Ms. Jocelyn's house. She loved spending time with Chelle and Mika, but this reminded her so much of her past. One minute she'd be happy, and the next it would all be taken away.

"Carla, I know you hear me calling you," India

said as she stepped into her room. "Why are you just sitting there?"

She couldn't tell her what she was thinking so she just got up off the bed.

"What's wrong?"

"Everything," she wanted to scream out, but instead said, "Nothing."

Despite being their older sister, India felt more like their mother. She sat on her sister's bed, reached out for her hand, and had her sit on the bed beside her. "Don't tell me nothing when I can see it's something. Remember I said you can always talk to me about anything."

Carla nodded and then started to cry. India hugged her. "I'm afraid," she revealed.

"Afraid?" she repeated the word, confused. "Afraid of what?" As India asked this, she lifted her sister's head up to look at her by putting a finger under her chin and lifting slightly.

After a minute, Carla managed to say, "Afraid that we'll be taken away."

India got it, but the only way any one would take her sisters was over her dead body.

Sandra came into the room and India motioned her over to her. She put her arms around them both as she looked at them. "No one will ever take you two away from me. Understand?"

"Yes," Sandra said, not really sure what was going on. Wiping her eyes with her hands, Carla nodded yes.

"Now get your coats. After I handle some business, I'm going to pick y'all back up and we are gonna watch some movies."

"Scary ones?" Carla asked excitedly.

"No, no, no. We always watch scary ones."

"Shut up, geek."

"Crybaby."

"Rather be a crybaby than a geek, Murtle," she teased calling her by the name of the Steve Urkel character on *Family Matters*.

India laughed.

"That ain't funny," Sandra pointed out.

India loved her sisters.

* * *

India looked at the photos of the men Mike had presented her with when she sat down in his club—Rock Jungle. After another shooting—this time inside—he was finally going to close the club down.

"Tired of fighting the city," he revealed to India after he broke the news to her. "Kids just too violent nowadays."

To that India agreed. Times were changing, but

she wasn't sitting in his office to talk about violence or the closing of his business. "What do you have for me?"

All business. Since meeting her, the lovely India had always been about business. He slid the photos across his desk to her. "Two of them." He separated the two. "Can only testify to your brother being their supplier. Not that they got it off of him directly. This one"—he tapped the picture with the pen he held in his hand—"actually got it off your brother. He was also the one that informed the police that the drugs were in a safety deposit box at the bank. From my sources, no drugs were found at the bank."

India only recognized the one that could tie her brother into a direct sale. The other two could only say the person would get it from LaRon. It was third party, but hearsay was admissible in federal court. All three would have to go. "What else do you have for me?"

"Right now I got people on the two. At any time, just give me the word, I can snatch them up. The other one is going to be slightly more difficult to touch. He's in the Beaver County Jail."

This did pose a huge problem. There was no way any of the three could testify in court. "Do you have any people at the jail?"

Mike shook his head no. "It's a small jail. Holds

around 440 to 500 prisoners' tops. Thought maybe I could find someone inside willing to make the hit, but it's a no go."

India sat there in deep thought. She knew she couldn't just break in the jail. Who did *that*? You usually broke someone out. And then it came to her. That is, if Mike could help her out. "Do you know what's holding him?"

He wasn't sure, but he could find out. He didn't know what good that would do. "I'm not following you."

"If it's a simple detainer holding him from his PO or a judge, I could draft up an order, get it faxed to the jail saying the detainer is lifted."

He got it. "I'll find out right now." He picked up his phone and called his connect within the feds. "Connie, pull up the file on that Latimore kid. Find out what's holding him. Yes, I'll hold on." He covered the phone. "If it's A-okay, I need a fax sent to Beaver County Jail granting his release. I need that kid on the streets." He listened and then smiled. "Thank you, Connie." He hung up. "She's gonna draft up his phony release. Has a federal hold."

"How long do you think this release will take?"

He shrugged. "She's very good at what she does. I'll get a call. Do you want me to have him picked up?"

Figuring that he wouldn't get in a car with her, she shook her head yes. "Have the other two picked up too."

"Want them all to disappear?" Owning a crematory came in handy.

Originally she thought that might be the best way, but a missing body didn't have the same effect as a dead one for all to see. A statement had to be made. There were too many people involved in his case. Everyone had to be made aware that if you snitched, you died. There was nowhere you could hide, and no one could protect you. That's the message she wanted to send.

Fourteen

Having a federal case simply changed his yellow card to a white one. There wasn't a feds-only pod at the ACJ. No bond was set, so after LaRon went in front of the district magistrate, he was returned to the ACJ. His new attorney appeared at the hearing, but he was curious as to why his normal attorney wasn't present. Because he returned to the jail at 2:10 p.m., he had to sit in a holding cell in Intake and wait for the changing of the guards and 3:00 count to clear—which usually didn't clear until a quarter to four. He managed to get back at 4:00 just in time to catch the breaking news of his attorney killing himself. As soon as the phone came on, he called his sister. She didn't answer. He called his woman and it went through. "I set up the calls last night. Why ain't you call all day?"

He explained the feds picking up his case and informed her of his attorney killing himself. Both things she already knew.

"Call my sis from the house phone." He waited while Deamber dialed India's cell. He could hear her answering machine when it picked up. "Wonder what the fuck she's up to."

"Did your visiting list go through?"

"I'll check after this call. Let me talk to my son."
At age four, LaRon Jr. was talking good. LaRon
missed the hell out of his family. The last two days
seemed like a week. Before he knew it, the
automated voice came on and announced there was
only a minute remaining. "I'll call you back after I
check the visiting list." He hung up and went to the
desk. "Can I check my visiting list?"

"Don't have access," the CO lied.

LaRon had no idea he'd been lied to by a man
who was just too lazy to do his job. He walked into
the gym, where a few of his people were. He passed
the tobacco off. "Roll something up, nigga." He
wanted to smoke before he tried to call his sis and
Deamber back. Some dude was shooting an
imaginary ball at an imaginary rim.

"The niggas gone," Tone told him.

He thought the nigga was playing.

"The feds got our shit, family."

They all knew that. A few more of their crew
had been called for court, and word soon spread
what was taking place.

"I'd rather do fed time than state," the nigga who
rolled up revealed. "Shit way different in the feds.
They treat you better. Feed you better."

Tone agreed by nodding his head. LaRon thought both of the niggas was crazy. He wasn't trying to do no time in anybody's prison.

This shit wasn't for him. He left after smoking, letting the niggas who did time before compare stories. He called his sister's number, and she picked up.

"What's good?" he asked her.

"Out here handling shit. Am I on your visiting list yet?"

"Tried to find out, but dude working the pod ain't got access to the computer."

The nigga on the phone next to him started yelling, calling the person he was talking to all types of name. "Stupid bitch! You's a dumb bitch. Why don't you shut the fuck up and listen to me." LaRon turned his back so he could hear his sister.

"I'm real busy right now, so I can't talk. I'll be down there as soon as I'm on the list."

He wanted to ask her what was up, but the phone calls, all of them, were recorded. He would have to wait. "I'll call you before lockup," he said before he hung up. He called his woman.and

"Who the fuck is Iesha Lockett?" Deamber asked.

"What?"

"Ieasha Lockett. She's on your visiting list."

If she would have said Iesha called or the two of them had words, he would have denied knowing the bitch. He had no comeback for this. He said the only thing he could think of. "What the fuck you talking about?"

"I called to see if we—me and India—was on your list, and the guard said, 'Yeah, and Iesha.' Who the fuck is she, LaRon?"

The last thing he was going to do was admit to having cheated with the girl. He really wasn't sure if he was going to let her come to see him. You were only allowed two visits a week. His sis and Deamber would take them up. Still, just in case, he put her on. He didn't know Deamber would find out. "I don't know."

"Oh, you don't know, huh?"

"Look, I don't got time for this bullshit. I don't know no motherfucking Iesha."

"Stop fuckin lyin'!"

"Who the fuck you yelling at?" LaRon asked as he decided to use the technique of the nigga beside him.

"Stupid white bitch," the nigga beside him yelled into the phone.

"I got serious shit going on and you ask me 'bout some bitch. You's about a dumb...."

"Thank you for using Technetics," the

automated voice said, ending the call.

LaRon was playing mad, but when he realized she hung up on him, he got upset for real.

He called her right back. As soon as she accepted, he yelled, "You bang on me?"

"Who the fuck is she, LaRon?"

"Yeah, you banged on me."

Deamber unsuccessfully tried not to cry. That he cheated on her in the past meant very little to her. The fact that they were now engaged is what hurt. She didn't respond.

He wanted to keep up with the dumb shit, but the sound of her crying cut it short. "I'll take her off."

It was hard enough dealing with him being gone. She wasn't about to deal with some other bitch. "LaRon, if I ain't enough for you, tell me."

After what she found out, he guessed she had a reason to say that. "She don't mean shit to me, baby. I'll take her off the list."

For now, that was enough. She hadn't gotten her answer, but she would.

When India got off the phone with her brother, she was nearing her destination. She knew Mike's help wasn't corning without a hidden agenda. She could never give him what he wanted, which was herself. Her career and family was her number one priority. Men had never interested her. It wasn't that she was gay, because women weren't her thing either. It's just her focus wasn't on a relationship. What no one knew is, despite her infrequent dates, India was still a virgin in every sense of the world. In fact, only two men could lay claim to having kissed her. Mike Astari was nice. He was also an attractive man in her eyes. What ended his chance wasn't the fact that he was Italian or in the mafia. He was married. That was sacred in her eyes. So the most he could get out of it was friendship.

As she got out of her car at the place he told her to meet him, she knew she had to let him know there was no future for them. He wasn't alone when she walked into the building. Sitting in steel folding chairs were the three men that turned out to be snitches. Mike was also seated, but he had a gun in his hand. He stood when she walked in.

"We've been waiting on you," Mike announced.

"Sorry to keep you waiting," she said as though it was a business meeting. She stopped when she was beside Mike, and took the gun he handed her.

The one who recognized her spoke. "India, I swear to God I wasn't going to snitch," Sap, the fat kid that used to eat at her table along with her brother said. She knew he was lying. There was nothing left of his pleas. She shot him dead in the center of his forehead, knocking him out of his seat. In rapid succession she fired four more times. All three of the snitches lay dead on the floor.

"I want them found. Put their bodies out so everyone knows that if you rat, you die," India instructed.

Mike watched the execution, detached. He'd killed his share of people over the years. Being the head of the Pittsburgh mafia, he wasn't used to taking orders from anyone. Yet, he nodded at her instructions as though he was her flunky. He had a surprise for her. "Someone has been following you, building a case against you."

She looked at Mike, confused.

He smiled. "Luckily, I had someone on the inside to reveal his actions. Bring him in." India watched as two men, obviously Mike's men, drag a seemingly unconscious and badly beaten man across the floor. One of the men punched the man in his ribs, evoking a moan out of him.

Through puffy and swollen eyes, the man looked at the bodies lying dead on the ground.

After years of seeing dead bodies, he had no trouble recognizing what the three were. He slowly raised his head to look at his executioner. He knew his time had come.

Something about the man's build jogged her

memory. And then he looked up. Her eyes got just as big as the condemned man's. Unable to stand on his feet, Det. Clyde Dexter could not believe his eyes.

India's heart raced.

Fifteen

Red watched as Shelly, a fiend from his hood, cooked up an ounce of the coke. He wasn't taking any chances of her fucking shit up. She said she knew what the fuck she was doing, but no one was taking a chance on messing up more than an ounce.

"I'm telling you, I can cook up a quarter bird at a time," the fiend bragged.

Joel wasn't feeling her talkative ass at all. Since they picked up the bitch, she hadn't shut the fuck up. "Shut the fuck up!"

Shelly cut her eyes at the short, high-yellow nigga and rolled her eyes. "His ass is evil."

The four sat in Dip's kitchen waiting on Shelly to show them if she was worthy of cooking up their shit. After their meeting with Andre from the North side, who set them up with a nigga he knew, they had the four parts of the city covered. Dip's BM and the kids were at the Ardmore Bowling Alley.

"Leave her alone, nigga," A.D. said. He had plans to be with Taylor. The sooner they got the shit done, the sooner he'd be with her.

"Fuck you, nigga, and this crackhead bitch," Joel said.

"I'm trying to bounce, homie. Chill."

Joel got up. He didn't see any sense of just sitting around watching the bitch. He called Sasha.

"Thank you," Shell said. Shit, she was doing them a favor. She got high, but that didn't mean they could disrespect her. She focused on doing the job they were going to pay her for.

In no time, she produced a solid ounce of hard. Dip put it on the scale. It came back twenty-eight grams—an ounce. She hadn't lost anything.

He broke a piece off. "Try that in the basement," he instructed.

She took it and did as she was told. She returned four minutes later, her pupils dilated and glazed. "It's melt."

Red set the bird, minus an ounce, in front of her. "Can you still cook now you high?"

"Hell yeah. Now it's on and poppin: Step back and watch a bitch whip up the best hard out this motherfucker."

They all did just that. The plan was to cook up twelve birds and take those to the ground.

Each side would get four birds each.

By the time his BM got back, they were finished. Dip remained with his BM, and that night the two renewed their sexual relationship.

* * *

With A.D. and Joel hooking up with their girls, Red was the only one faithful to his motto: "M-o-b, money over bitches." He had no steady and didn't want one. To Red, all a bitch wanted was to dig in a nigga's pockets. He didn't trust females. When he wanted some pussy, he called the massage parlor. Phillipinos, Chinese, Russians—you name it, he had them. And he hadn't even left the United States. His latest conquest was African bitches. Not bitches who were black African Americans—straight from Africa. Model type Africans that spoke with heavy accents. All he had to do was call the old white woman who lived out Monroeville and tell her his choice. He'd tell her what hotel he was in, and forty-five minutes to an hour later, a woman would be at his door.

He was in the Hilton downtown waiting on his African. Tomorrow and until he got rid of the four birds, he'd be on his grind and have no time for pussy. This night he was on some *Mandingo* shit. A soft knock on the door got him up. He peered through the peephole and smiled. He opened the door. "What country are you from?"

"Zambia," she said as she stepped in.

He shut the door. You look like that model from Africa. "What's her name?"

"Iman," she said. "And that bitch has nothing on me." She let her dress fall to the floor.

She had nothing on underneath. She slowly turned showing him her plump ass, flat stomach, busty tits, and shaved pussy.Red had to agree.

"Now get out them clothes and fuck me."

Her accent did it for him. He couldn't get out of his clothes fast enough.

* * *

Taylor had never been so scared in her life. She had no one to blame but herself. How could she have been so stupid? Despite enjoying being with A.D., she didn't know shit about him, not even his real name. She prided herself on not being a common hood rat, yet she'd done some hood rat shit. She was pregnant. As she stared down at the positive sign on the pregnancy stick she had in her hand, she wanted to burst into tears. That wouldn't help matters though. All she needed to hear is some foul shit come out of A.D.'s mouth. "It ain't mine!" and it would really be officially some hood rat drama. She laughed as she thought of the girls on the *Maury* show.

"Uh-huh, Maury, I am one million percent sure he my baby's daddy. Read the test, Maury."

Maury gets up to retrieve the test results, pulls them out of the envelope, and says, "In the case of baby's name to be determined, you are . . ."

Taylor imagined herself jumping up and saying, "I told you, beep, beep."

"Not the father."

A.D. would start to dance and Taylor would run off the stage busted.

Naw, that wouldn't be her fate. She hadn't cheated, but A.D. didn't know that. She heard him as he let himself in. She gave him his own key a week before.

"Babe," he called out.

"In the bedroom."

He came in and smiled. "You horny?"

She had to smile. With him, she was always horny. "More than that, I'm pregnant." She had no easy to tell him.

He'd been trying to have a baby since fourteen. "Real talk?"

Taylor nodded yes.

He didn't know what to say, so he just stood there and looked at her.

"What's your real name?" It was kind of stupid

to ask, but it popped in her head. Besides, the silence made her nervous.

"Anthony Davis. Why?"

She shrugged. "I'm pregnant by you. You'd think I'd know your name."

She didn't seem too thrilled to be having his baby. "What's wrong? Why ain't you happy?"

"On top of me not knowing your name, I did not plan to get pregnant, and with us not talking about a child. My happiness is yet to be determined."

"We ain't plan shit, but I'm happy as a motherfucker," he answered.

"For real?" The possibility of raising a child on her own terrified her. Shit wasn't easy supporting herself. Another mouth to feed and body to clothe would be an added burden that she didn't know if she could bear.

"Real talk, mami ." He hugged her and rubbed her stomach.

His touch excited her. He was so close she could smell him. "I'm horny." Music to his ears—so was he!

***

The exchange between Joel and Sasha didn't go as smoothly. Not only was he not too happy about having a baby, but also Sasha wasn't too happy about the fact her Rican girl Maria was having his baby too.

"Told your ass to use a rubber."

He hated rubs. Shit didn't feel as good. "Both you bitches should've been on birth control. It's cool though. We'll get an abortion." He reached in his pocket and pulled out a roll of money. "How much that shit cost?"

"Nigga, how the fuck I know? I don't go out getting abortions on the regular."

He counted out a thousand dollars. "It don't cost more than that."

He left, and Sasha's strong resolve crumbled. She hoped he'd be happy, that maybe he'd make her wifey. It was cool though. She had to pull it together. She didn't need a baby anyways. That would only mess up her clubbing and smoking. At least he paid for the abortion and she didn't have to get it from the next nigga.

Joel left straight from Sasha's and went to Maria's house. Since their threesome, he hit it off a few times. That shit was over now. "Get an abortion," he ordered as soon as she opened the door. He had the thousand in his hand, not too happy about losing out on two stacks.

Maria, a devout catholic, backed away as though

he held a gun in his hand. She crossed herself several times and began to speak in Spanish.

The shit scared the fuck out of Joel. He thought she was putting some voodoo shit on him.

Her eyes opened. "I don't believe in abortion, papi. Me and my baby will be fine without you." Before he knew what she was doing, she shut and locked the door. "Your money is no good here," she told him through the door.

Her bizarre reaction scared him from knocking on her door again. He did not believe in God. In between the Spanish shit he didn't understand, he caught mention of the Virgin Mary, Jesus, and God. There was some shit even he didn't fuck around with. He'd convince her later to get an abortion. Right then, all he wanted was a drink. He called his boy A.D.

"People, you know both them bitches is knocked. Meet me at Riverside, I need a drink." He hung up. He knew his boy was having a baby and was happy about it. The nigga even was talking about marrying Taylor. Fuck all that.

A.D. pulled up a block from the bar on East Carson and was stopped by a cop telling him to make a left turn. He made the turn wondering what was going on, and then he saw Joel's car crashed into parked cars. He stopped in the middle of the street and raced past the surprised cop.

(A few minutes earlier)

Joel thought maybe having a baby wasn't so bad by the time he got on the West End Bridge. He'd call Sasha as soon as he got a drink. Then he said fuck it and called her right then. He had her call Maria on three-way. "I'm sorry," he said simply. "I want y'all to have the babies. And you bitches better act right now that y'all are having my seed."

Maria crossed herself. Her prayer for him to come around and accept the baby was heard. "Yes, papi."

Sasha couldn't have been happier. "Okay, daddy."

He smiled and looked to his left.

"Remember me, nigga?" Dude in the car beside him asked.

Joel did remember him. It was one of the niggas from Sandcastle. From the news Joel knew only two niggas died that day. He stepped on the gas as shots rang out. He took one in the shoulder, which wasn't fatal. But the one in the neck was. He crashed into some parked cars.

The airbags deployed, but it was too late. Joel was dead.

Hearing the shots, both women on the phone began to scream.

As he came upon the scene, A.D. was restrained by a cop. He could see his boy pinned in his seat by the airbags. "That's my bro. That's my best friend. Let me go. Get the fuck off me!" he screamed to no avail. "Aaaaaaaahhhhhhh!" he screamed so loud and with so much pain, even the cop holding him shed a tear.

Sixteen

India couldn't believe the beat-up man was not only a cop, but also the cop she was slowly starting to despise. He was the cause for her brother being locked up. Although killing him wouldn't end her brother's problems, she'd get some satisfaction out of it. Yet as he stared intently into her eyes, she hesitated—not because he was a cop, she cared very little about that. He could easily be killed and she could have Mike cremate him—no evidence. But still she hesitated. Why? "Sit him in a chair and leave us."

It wouldn't be the first time Mike had to kill a cop. In fact, Robert Manuel's ashes were still in a vase at the crematory. He had outlived his usefulness. The cop before him now could go just as easily. He wasn't sure about leaving her alone, but the cop was busted up pretty good and unarmed. If the man tried something, he was confident she could handle herself. He left as she requested.

Clyde clutched at his midsection, but he didn't take his eyes off of her. "This goes deeper"—he struggled with his words, spitting out blood in the process—"than I thought."

Why did she have the urge to go to him? To comfort him? "Why were you building a case against me?"

He shook his head from side to side. "I wasn't, I was trying to protect you." Hearing his words, she immediately wondered why he was trying to protect her.

"The feds thought you were the brains behind your brother's operation. I was trying to convince them it wasn't possible." It took some time for him to get his words out. "I see now that I was wrong." He paused. "But even still, I'd tell them you don't have anything to do with it."

She stared at him, confused.

"All my life I wanted to be a cop. Thought I'd be able to help out blacks. You know, cut down on police brutality. My job is to arrest people, put people—white, black, yellow, etc.—in jail if they break the law. But then I met you. From the first moment I laid eyes on you in that E room, I've been in love with you." He saw her expression change, and he smiled in spite of the pain. "I know it's crazy, but it's true. I never had the courage to approach you, but one thing I do know is I never loved anyone as much as I love you," he proclaimed as tears ran down his cheeks. He passed out.

* * *

"He's starting to come around."

He recognized the voice of his partner, but Donald wasn't dead. He opened his eyes to the bright light. At least he wasn't in hell burning up.

"Clyde," he heard someone say.

"Jesus," Lloyd said weakly.

"He's delusional," someone else said.

Clyde's eyes adjusted to the light. He recognized his partner and saw the man in white and a few more people—two women and a man. He wasn't dead. He hurt, had trouble breathing, but he was alive. "I'm alive," he said in disbelief.

"Just barely, buddy. Just barely," Donald said.

The last thing he remembered was passing out. Why hadn't she killed him? Did she try and fail? Was he shot? "How many times was I shot?" he asked.

"Shot?" his partner said. "You weren't shot. Beat up pretty good. Was there a gun involved? Do you know who did this?"

He knew. What he didn't know is why and what took place after he passed out.

* * *

(Before Clyde passed out)

Mike saw the cop as he slid from the chair to the ground. He heard no retort from the gun she held. In fact, the gun never raised from her side to point at the cop. Mike realized he went too far and could not hear what was said. When the cop fell, he made his way to India, stopping to stand beside her. "You want me to finish him off?"

India was still a little shocked from hearing Clyde's words. They weren't a desperate attempt from a condemned man, willing to say anything to save his life. His words reached a part of her no man had ever come close to reaching: her heart. "Mike, you cannot kill this man."

"Why not?" he asked.

She turned and faced Mike. "Do you know how you feel about me? How you'd do anything for me?"

He nodded.

She dropped the gun to the floor and bent to Clyde. "I feel that way for him, the same way." That revelation might seal her own fate, but she had to try to save him.

Hearing her proclaim her love for another man nearly drove him to empty the entire clip into the unconscious man's body. "If he lives, what makes you think he won't tell what he witnessed or who roughed him up?"

"He won't," she said.

* * *

"How did I get here?"

"A woman brought you in. She's standing in the hallway. I gave her the benefit of the doubt. She claims she's a friend."

Clyde's heart raced. Could it be possible? "Let her in."

When the woman walked in, Clyde tried to figure out who she was. How did she find him? And then India stepped in the room.

"Ma'am." Clyde held up his hand.

"Hey," she said nervously. Was this man's declaration of love real?

"I'm a friend of his as well."

Donald thought the woman looked familiar, but he looked at his partner.

This was better than a dream. Better than being in heaven. He couldn't believe it. He reached out his hand and India took it. "Leave us please."

The room cleared out, leaving just the two of them. "You know I'll have to quit."

"That's okay," she told him as she smiled. "I got plenty of money."

He had so many questions to ask her. But only one seemed important. "Is this real?"

She kissed him softly on his bruised and busted lips. "As real as it gets. I love you." Nothing else mattered to him.

* * *

India stood behind Deamber, who was sitting on the small stool smiling at her brother.

She hadn't had a chance to talk to him yet, choosing to let Deamber and her nephew talk. It was their first visit.

LaRon caught the news of the killings of members of his crew. He wasn't stupid. It just wasn't a coincidence the niggas were dead. What had him perplexed was why? Somehow he figured his sister would give him the answers he wanted. He was anxious to talk to his sister. "Put India on."

"What's up, Bro?"

"You know." They said nothing for a few seconds. "Caught the news."

She wasn't taking a chance even on the phone they had to talk on because of the plexiglass separating them. "Shit happens—niggas being niggas."

He nodded. There was mention of an investigation being conducted and the mistaken release of a federal prisoner, on the news. He had his answer.

"So what else is good?"

"Dip hollered at me with your paper and I moved that other shit."

He'd been worried about his money. When all this shit was over, he was retiring. He had had enough.

"Oh, I'm in love," she said casually.

He twisted his lips up and said, "Yeah, right."

"Seriously," she said.

"Stop playing," he told her, but then he looked at her face and could tell she was serious. "With who?"

That was something she wasn't willing to say. Not just yet. "You know him. That's all I'm going to say."

That wasn't enough for him, but a guard on the other side, their side, knocked on the glass on the door to let them know the hour-long visit was over. It went too fast. And he didn't get the chance to find out who the nigga his sis was fucking with was.

SEVENTEEN

Despite the two no longer being together as a couple, Joel's mother and father sat together with the remaining surviving siblings of his, in the first row of chairs.

The turnout was of normal size, close to 150 mourners, most of whom were hustlers and bangers from his West side hood. If he wasn't well liked, he was well respected and feared. The funeral was held in Elliot.

A.D. stood at his boy's casket as tears rolled down his face. He couldn't believe Joel was gone. Shit was just about to jump off for them. This was the come up the two had been waiting on. They were supposed to do it big together.

Sasha and Maria sat together. Shit just got a lot harder for them both. The elation they both felt at the news Joel was going to take responsibility for his kids was short lived. That he had no children prompted both women to have the babies—especially after talking to A.D., who vowed in honor of his boy, he'd take on the financial responsibility for both kids.

"I'll take care of them like they are my own," he promised.

Since the two had been like brothers, he felt in a sense that the kids would be his nephews or nieces. Joel's mother, two sisters, father, and brother had been elated that Joel had kids on the way, despite the fact that it was different women.

Taylor attended as well. She was there for her girl, but also for her man that was having a difficult time dealing with his boy's death. They spent the last few days leading up to the funeral together, and most of it was spent with her trying to console him. What ended up happening was, he cried himself to sleep and she lay there deep in thought.

She knew what he did, knew the dangers of it, and it worried her silly. Raising a child on her own minus the child's father wasn't a fate she wanted for herself or unborn child. The prospect terrified her and prompted her to make the decision to talk to A.D.

She walked up and took his hand and kissed it tenderly. He had no idea who killed his boy. All he wanted was revenge. He owed that to his boy.

The viewing lasted two hours, and then everyone took the drive to the cemetery. As Joel's casket was lowered into the ground, a piece of A.D.'s soul died. Many would wonder, including himself, if Joel hadn't been killed, would things have turned out the same.

Would A.D. have done the unthinkable? It was a question debated in the streets of the West side for years to come.

* * *

Taylor wasn't the only young black watching something political in her life. For the first time, A.D. sat on the floor between her legs and even he was watching the special news coverage. Neither could believe it. It was the coverage they thought would never happen in their lifetime. A black man was running for President of the United States: Barack Obama.

Neither had heard of the man before this day. Listening to him speak now, both dared to believe it would happen.

"You know they gonna try to kill him," A.D. pointed out. "He ain't gonna live to see the election."

Taylor shook her head in disagreement. An optimist, she believed he would. And not only that, but also that she'd see a black man in office. "He's gonna do it."

A.D. had run the circuit of juvenile lockup and

seen his share of racist acts. That white people would be okay with a black man running the country was hard to believe. "I don't know."

"You just make sure you vote for him come election time. Matter of fact, we are going together."

At twenty-three, A.D. had never voted in his life, not even for class president in his school. "Am I demo . . . ?" he paused, confused, having no idea of the word he was searching for. He had heard it before, but it wasn't a part of his vocabulary.

"Democrat?" Taylor said hopefully. "It's Democrat or Republican, babe."

"The nigga running for president is which one?"

"The black man?"

"Nigga, black man, brother, whatever you want to call him. Which one is he?"

Taylor smiled and shook her head. Later she'd get around to not calling Obama or any black "nigga." Right now she was just happy he showed an interest. "He's Democrat."

"Then I'm a motherfucking Democrat. Is that right?"

"Yeah."

"Democrat."

Later that day while getting his haircut, A.D. told everyone in the barber shop, "I'm a Democrat, nigga."

One young thirteen-year-old waiting to get a haircut said, "What set they from, my nigga?"

Several of the men, including A.D., laughed. None admitted that most had learned the word because of the coverage of Barack's announcement.

"My political party, nigga," A.D. told him.

Youngin' went back to watching the BET top 10 countdown. He didn't know what the nigga was talking about.

A stir in the city and the cities around the country began on that day. For a moment, it gave blacks hope—hope that things would finally change. But for A.D., it was the beginning to the end.

He focused on grinding like he never had before. He had his kids, his boys' kids, and Taylor to provide for. Selling drugs became his number one priority.

* * *

Dip's relationship with his wife began to suffer because of his constant grind. He saw less and less of his wife and more of Donna, his daughter's mom. He got Donna pregnant when she was only fifteen, and she had their daughter at sixteen. She was a woman now—a sexy-ass woman that was a freak in the bedroom. Kim, Dip's wife, started out as a freak, but after the birth of their son, who was now nearing two, and their marriage, Kim's sexual appetite had diminished. Oh, he still got some, but missionary and doggy was as wild as she got. Getting some head was out of the question. What did she expect from him? To go from nothing off limits to two to three times a week and basic sex? Dip was sexually frustrated, driven into the arms of another woman. Still, he didn't expect his wife to do what she did.

"It's like that, Roger?"

He'd just gotten out of the shower after spending the night out with Donna. It was a little after noon. He was naked, standing in front of the mirror shaving. He turned to face his wife, "What the fuck you talking about?"

"Who the fuck is this bitch?"

He ducked as she tossed the photos at him. One landed in the sink and he picked it up. It was him at a restaurant with Donna. There were several more on the floor. One was of his daughter—the one he never told his wife about. That he was busted didn't faze him. What had him pissed was the fact that someone had obviously been following him. Before he'd gotten out of the game, she was there. Donna was his bitch and then wifey, long before Kim was his wife. She knew about the streets. He'd even told her he was getting back in the game. "Goofy bitch," he screamed as he slapped her to the floor. "You hired someone to follow me knowing I hustle."

Kim couldn't believe he had hit her. Not that it hadn't happened in the past. He wasn't going to switch it up and act like she was to blame. Mindless of the swelling that began immediately under her eye, she jumped up and attacked her husband.

Caught off guard by his wife's actions, Dip took a step back. Not a second too soon either—her nails nearly raked across his face. He gripped Kim up, and she tried to bite his chest. He spun her around and slipped on the water from the shower, and they both went down hard. Kim screamed as she came down awkwardly, with all Dip's weight on top off her, her shoulder pushed out of place.

"Daddy!" his two-year-old son said as he stared fearfully at them both.

Dip rolled off of Kim, causing her to yell out in pain. He reached for her, but she kicked him.

"Don't fuckin touch me! Nigga, you can hit on me and I bore your seed." Tears rolled down her face. She sat up in obvious pain as her left arm hung loosely at her side. She tried to cradle it, but that caused even more pain.

Seeing that his wife was seriously hurt and the fact that his son was there staring at them, his anger left him. "Let me get on some clothes and I'll get you to the hospital."

Kim walked gingerly past her crying son.

"Can't you tell him you alright? You just gonna walk by him?"

She walked down the steps and Dip scooped up his son.

"Stop crying, boy" he told his son. "Mommy is okay." He could hear her talking on the phone. Probably called one of her sisters. Every time something jumped off, her sisters were the first one she called. "Why you got to call your family when we get into it?" He wanted to tell her to go live with one of them nosey bitches, but shit already got out of control. He took his son with him into their bedroom and got dressed.

He regretted slapping her, but she didn't know what he was doing during the time he'd been watched. Thankfully he hadn't killed anyone or done any transactions. He'd apologize and spend more time with her. Donna was fun, but Kim had his heart. After he dressed, he carried his son down the steps. "Where you at?" he called out to his wife. The front door was wide open. He knew this bitch didn't ride to the hospital without him.

He went to the door and saw she was sitting behind the wheel of her car. He could tell she was still crying. He activated the alarm, set his son down, and closed the door. When he turned back around, he saw the first of two police cars drive onto his property. Kim got out of her car.

"That's the last time you put your motherfucking hands on me," she shouted.

"Cops, Daddy. Cops," two-year-old De'Shawn said.

Dip couldn't believe she had called the police. His face hardened, but he stood still. There was nothing he could do. Luckily he didn't bring his strap with him.

Three cops got out of the cars. One stood talking to Kim, and the other two made their way over to him.

"What's going on, sir?" one of the cops asked.

He watched as Kim talked to the cop, and he knew the outcome. The cop that was talking to his wife made his way over to them.

"Mr. Underwood, you are under arrest for spousal abuse. Place your hands behind your back," he ordered.

Dip did as the man said, never taking his eyes off of his wife.

Only a small part of her regretted calling the police on her husband. She couldn't believe it had come to this.

"Do you need medical attention, ma'am?" She nodded her head no.

Neither knew this was only the beginning to the end. Soon their lives would be flipped upside down.

EIGHTEEN

The backlash from the deaths of the FBI informants created more pressure from the attorney general. He wanted LaRon in the worst way. He had everyone trying to find out how the informants were discovered, and more importantly, how a fax was sent from the federal headquarters to Beaver County Jail. That the dealer could possibly have someone on the inside was mind-blowing. He refused to believe that, but somehow security had been breached.

LaRon was moved from 4-A to 6-D, a maximum-security pod, at 3:30, his fourth day in the jail. Usually it took at least ten days before someone moved off of the orientation pods. When he got to 6-D, he saw a lot of familiar faces and even one enemy.

"What's good, homie?"

The nigga who greeted him was once a part of his team. He branched off and started doing his own thing. The last LaRon heard, the nigga got busted with some bricks of dope and a chopper. He clapped him and whispered to the nigga, "I got to handle something. Watch my back." He went to the guard's desk, handed the man his card, and was assigned a cell on the lower tier:107 cell.

"I'll get you a mattress before the night's over," the guard said. "Got to find it." He knew if he called out over the intercom for it, no one would turn it in.

LaRon took his bag to his cell, speaking to those he knew while still keeping his eyes on the dude he once had a beef with. Dude hadn't attempted to get up from the spade table, but LaRon had no intention of waiting on dude to say something. He headed straight to the table dude was sitting at. "Let me holla at you a minute."

It was a clear challenge, one that didn't go unnoticed by the other prisoners on the block.

Everyone waited.

Craig knew it was corning. He'd once robbed one of LaRon's dudes. There was no way he couldn't accept. Despite being a few inches taller than LaRon, LaRon was a solid 210 pounds. The guy set his cards on the table and stood up.

LaRon followed him to his cell. Craig put his towel up on the window for a curtain and LaRon stepped in and closed the door.

Craig had his own crew of niggas he rolled with on the pod. They'd all seen the coverage on the nigga that just stepped on the pod, and some even knew LaRon. They knew this was a fight that had to be, one in which no one could jump in. There was just as many niggas who'd fight with LaRon, if not more.

Inside the cell, LaRon and Craig started swinging as soon as the doors closed. Craig knew how to fight and landed some nice blows. His problem was that he lacked any real power to slow LaRon down. Then to top it off, LaRon had power with his. The hook LaRon hit Craig with weakened his knees and caused Craig to stumble back into the desk. He shook his head, trying to shake off the dizziness, but LaRon took advantage, landing a two-punch combo that made Craig reach out and attempt to grab him. He saw his move, took a few steps back, and caught Craig cleanly with a right uppercut. He went down. LaRon thought about stumping the nigga, but he stepped over him and pushed the button to open the door. He walked out.

Those who knew the fight was going on and could see into the cell, saw Craig trying to get to his feet. The guard at the desk had no idea a fight had just taken place. Although he won the fight, LaRon knew that it might not be over. He went to his cell, looked in the mirror, and checked his face. He had a knot over his eye, but other than that, he was cool.

"LaRon Jones, they want you down in Intake,"

the guard told him through the intercom.

Getting a page like that was never good—especially this late in the day. He waved the dude over he spoke to when he first stepped on the block. He gave him all of his tobacco and told him he could fire up something while he was gone.

"You need your card," the guard told him when he got to the door.

Getting his card, he had to be leaving the jail. It was after four o'clock, so he knew it wasn't court. Another guard awaited him at the outside door, leading to the elevators. He had no clue what was up, and he still didn't know even after he saw the two federal marshals waiting on him.

"Over here, Mr. Jones."

"What's going on?"

One of the marshals grabbed ahold of his arm and guided him to where he could kneel on a seat so he could get shackled. He stood up and was handcuffed. They still didn't give him an answer as they led him out to their car.

Patrick Tomlin, state attorney general, was pissed. Never in all the years of him prosecuting a case had so much misfortune taken place: evidence turning up missing, witnesses turning up dead, breach of security. Heads were going to spin when he got to the bottom of it—and he would. Right now he had to do something that he absolutely hated.

"Sir, they've arrived," his security informed him.

His jacket, as well as his tie, lay discarded on his chair. For the last nine hours, since eight o'clock in the morning, he'd been going over every bit of evidence they had with his team against LaRon Jones. At this hour, he had to admit defeat. He got up and went to the conference room.

"Where is my attorney?"

LaRon looked like the common thug Tomlin had put away for the past twenty-three years he was the AG, but LaRon was much smarter. He'd covered his tracks well. And somehow he infiltrated Tomlin's ranks. That, more than anything, made LaRon Jones a lifelong enemy. Tomlin could prolong things, try to see if any others would step up to testify, but after the murdered bodies of the three informants turned up, he doubted that strategy would work. "Leave us," he told the two marshals. They obeyed instantly. He pulled up a chair so he was sitting directly in front of LaRon, their knees touching.

"My attorney."

"Shut up, you murderous, drug-dealing maggot!" Tomlin ordered, barely able to contain his rage. "I want you to listen to me and listen good.

When you are walking down the streets, I'll be watching; when you are on the phone, I'll be listening; when you are in your bed sleeping and dreaming, I'm the boogey man. From this day forward, I'll be the eyes in the back of your head." After speaking, he got up and left.

LaRon had no clue what the fuck dude was talking about. The marshals came back in and escorted him back to the jail. He had his new attorney's house and cell number. He couldn't wait to call him. The shit the state attorney did was illegal. That might help his case.

He was in one of the Intake holding tanks with about fifteen other prisoners, waiting to go back to his pod. He wished they'd hurry the fuck up and come take him back upstairs. He needed the phone and a cigarette.

"LaRon Jones," a guard who came and opened the door called out.

LaRon got up, thinking "about time." "Yeah."

"You need anything from upstairs?"

"Huh?"

"You're released. Do you need anything from your pod?"

"Released?" he said, confused. The word just refused to sink in.

"The feds dropped their case against you," he

explained. "If you don't need anything from your pod, you can get dressed and you'll be out of here."

Besides some legal shit, personal care products, two letters, some pictures from Deamber, and the tobacco, he had nothing up there. And he wasn't going up there to get none of that shit. "Naw, I'm cool."

"Well come on and get dressed."

"Let me get them Jordans, homie. I know you ain't gonna need them."

LaRon had no clue who the nigga was that asked for his $200 new Jordans. It really didn't matter. "Kick off yours, homie," he told the nigga as he stepped out of his Jordans. He didn't mind going out in the blue jailhouse bobos.

"Keep your head up, youngster," the grateful recipient of the shoes said. He knew he could sell the shoes for a lot of commissary items. He had a small bit to do and no money.

"You too." LaRon stepped out in a daze. Even after he put his clothes on, he thought at any moment they were going to tell him it was all a joke and to put back on his jail reds.

Once he was dressed, he was put in another cell, along with more prisoners waiting to get out. It wasn't a long wait.

"Listen for your names."

When his name was called, he realized he was actually shaking. He stepped up to the desk for his property that he was not allowed to have when they brought him in: wallet, phones, keys, and ten dollars in cash.

"Here is a check," LaRon said to the guard who had looked out for him, handing over a check to the man.

"Damn!" the guard exclaimed when he noticed the amount. He showed the guard seated to his right. "This is more than I got in my bank account. Maybe I'm in the wrong line of work."

LaRon smiled as he took his things, including the check. "Maybe you are," he said. He went and put his back against the wall, waiting for the last person to get her property. Several females were getting out.

"Follow me."

Some prisoners, after serving a jail sentence, carried plastic bags of shit. LaRon was one of the few that had nothing. He cut on his phone in the elevator.

"Wait until you are outside the jail to use those phones," the escorting guard said.

It was a short ride on the elevator, and an even shorter walk through the visitor's waiting room and out the door. He stepped out and fired up a Newport.

Nothing ever tasted so good.

Those who smoked that didn't have any, asked him for one. He gave the whole pack up. He called his sister.

India nearly ignored the call when her phone rang and her brother's name popped up. She knew he took his phones in with him. Why his name would be popping up when he was in jail, she didn't know. When it rang for the fourth time, she answered, "Hello."

"They dropped the charges. I'm out."

India screamed so loud, she scared Clyde, who was seated beside her. The two were sitting in the living room in India's condo, watching a movie. He'd resigned that very day as a detective. Carla and Sandra came running into the living room. "Where are you?"

"Outside of the jail."

Living downtown, a short distance from the jail, India jumped up and said, "I'll be there in five minutes." She hung up. She couldn't believe it. "That was my brother. He's out. They dropped the charges!"

Clyde figured that's what would end up happening once those supposed to testify against LaRon were killed. Other than their testimony, there was really nothing incriminating against him. No one expected all three witnesses to end up dead. Carla and Sandra screamed as they jumped up and down excitedly.

"You go get your brother. I'll call you later." Clyde was still pretty banged up, with two cracked ribs, but he could still drive.

"Don't move. I told you I'd take care of you and I will. Besides, my brother is going to want to meet you." She paused because the two knew each other quite well by now. "You know what I mean. Wait right here. I'll be right back." She left out with her two sisters, who refused to wait at the house.

LaRon allowed a few people that got out to use his phone. When he saw his sister's car pull up, he gave it to the dude and told him he could keep it. It was the Cricket that he had bought right before he got knocked. He'd get his numbers out of his other phone and toss it in the trash. His younger sisters jumped out of the car and ran to him. He got on one knee and hugged them both.

India got out as well with tears in her eyes. She hugged her brother. "Told you I'd get you out."

He held her tightly. He never doubted it. "Who is this nigga you supposed to be in love with?" he asked. That shit was bugging him.

She knew he'd want to know. "He's at the house waiting on you."

LaRon walked to the car, not believing that not only did his sister have a man, a first in her life, but also that she was in love. Before he got knocked, she hadn't said shit about a man. "Do I know him?"

India smiled and pulled out, making an illegal U-turn. "Yes and no."

He didn't have long to wait. "Deamber and the kids are on their way to your house," he said, and then added. "Balil too."

"I know she was happy."

She was, but not as happy as he was. He turned to face his two sisters. "How do y'all like your family now after all of this?"

"Wouldn't change it for nothing in the world." Sandra said.

"Nope," Carla agreed, for once.

None of them would. Despite everything, they always had each other.

* * *

LaRon froze at the sight of the nigga he had fantasized about killing. The nigga he blamed for all his problems. His sister couldn't be serious. He looked at her, waiting for an explanation.

With her brother getting out so unexpectedly, India had no real time to prepare for how she was going to explain Clyde being in her life, so she started from the beginning of his revelation of love.

LaRon couldn't believe he witnessed three dead bodies on the ground and he hadn't snitched. Even more surprising than that was that Mike allowed the cop to live. "Mike let you live?"

It was Clyde who answered. "Yeah, he let me live. In return I can't pay him back for the ass kicking he and his men put on me. Oh, and by the way, he only listened to her 'cuz he's in love with her."

"He's not in love with me," India said.

Even LaRon knew that was a lie. She loved the fact that Clyde was jealous. It made him even cuter.

Before LaRon could say anything, the door burst open and in walked his woman and kids. His brother Balil wasn't far behind. This is where he needed to be—with his family. As he held his youngest, he announced his plans: "I'm done hustling."

That was one thing India had planned on talking to her brother about. He had more than enough money. Soon it all would be in a Swiss bank. It ended sooner than she thought it would.

It was all over. Or was it . . .

PART TWO

NINETEEN

After spending several hours locked up, Dip posted the $1,000 bond on his $10,000, 10 percent bond. He was told to stay away from his wife for seventy-two hours, at which time they'd have a hearing to determine if a longer PFA (protection from abuse) order would be granted. For Dip, one wasn't necessary. He had no intention of dealing with his wife again.

When she filed a PFA against him, she should have put in the divorce papers because shit was a wrap. When he got out, Donna was the one that came and picked him up.

"Finished with her," he announced when he got in the car.

"Oh yeah?" Donna didn't say more than that because she knew they both were on some mad shit. As soon as they got over their anger, they'd be right back together. She'd had huge fights with a few of her exs, even Dip, and always got over it.

"What the fuck is wrong with you?" he asked, thinking she had an attitude.

"Nothing, babe. You know I love you, but so

does your wife. I'll get in where I fit in. You know I play my part."

She always had, and initially that's what attracted him to her. Kim had always been the opposite. He always had to work at her 'cuz shit never went easy with them. It took him five and a half months to get some pussy. He wanted so bad to yell, "Fuck that bitch!" but that's really not how he felt. He smiled. "You know me too fuckin' good."

Donna smiled too. "Nigga, we were each other's first love. I know everything about you."

Dip looked up and noticed his surroundings. "Where are you going?"

"Taking your ass home to your wife and son. It's time to tell her about me and your daughter."

That didn't seem like a good idea for a number of reasons. He had no idea how Kim would take it and the PFA was in effect. If she called the cops and said he'd violated the order, he'd be taken right back to jail, and this time he wouldn't be allowed to post bond. "I don't know about this."

"Call her blocked and tell her you are on your way home. If she hangs up on you, she obviously is still mad. If she talks, well, you know."

He pushed star 72 before he dialed his wife's cell number. She picked up on the second ring. "Are you at the house?"

His question, his voice, came as a surprise to her. She regretted calling the police, but she wasn't about to put up with him hitting her. "At home. Why?"

Donna was right. "I'll be there in a little bit. We have to talk." He hung up. "Where are you going?" In order to get to his house, they were supposed to go straight. Donna made a left.

"It's time for her to meet your daughter as well."

He figured that much was true. They only had a short ride to go to pick up their daughter. She was standing in the McDonald's parking lot with a group of girls and two to three boys. She jumped in the back and playfully ran her hands over her dad's hair.

"Hey, old man," she greeted him.

"I'ma old man your ass, alright. Who was them boys?"

Angie shrugged her shoulders. "I don't know them ugly boys," she said as she sat back.

"Don't have me beat your little ass. Remember what I said."

His daughter rolled her eyes. "Who tells their kid they can't date until they die? Where they do that at?"

Donna laughed because she knew that if he had it his way, he'd have it that way.

TOMORROW'S NOT PROMISED 2

* * *

Their son was asleep in his room, and Kim sat anxiously in the living room waiting on her husband. She didn't get up when she heard the front door open. At the sight of the woman and girl, she was glad she didn't get up. It was the same woman in the pictures the investigator had taken: the woman her husband was cheating with. This was definitely the last straw. While she waited on him, she realized she was wrong for hiring a private investigator. She was going to tell him how sorry she was, but after this disrespect, it was over.

On some real shit, he loved his wife, and realized it as soon as he stepped into the house and saw her sitting there. He wanted to go to her and hug her. Her change in expression stopped him. He had to talk and talk fast. "Before you explode, I want you to hear me out," he began. "Long before I met you, I used to be involved with Donna. Our relationship ended, but not before we had our daughter, Angela."

Kim couldn't believe it. He always told her he didn't have any kids.

"Our relationship didn't end on good terms, and Roger was so entrenched in the streets at the time, that when I found out I was pregnant, I chose not to tell him. When our daughter turned nine, she told me she wanted to meet her dad. She's fourteen now," Donna added.

Kim calculated in her head the years. He found out a year and a half after they got together.

"At first, I was afraid to tell you. I knew how important it was to you that I didn't have any other children from another woman. As time passed, I thought it wasn't important."

"Wasn't important?"

It was a bad choice of words. He couldn't explain it. "I was wrong and I was wrong for putting my hands on you. If a nigga put his hands on my daughter, I'd kill him. You have my word, I'll never put my hands on you again."

Hearing his vow had little impact on her decision. She loved her husband with all her heart. She looked at his daughter and could see the similarities in both his children. "Is this it?"

He knew what she meant and so did Donna, who was the one that answered. "Yes, it is, Kim. I'll be the first one to say I'm sorry."

Kim looked at her husband, who nodded his head up and down.

"Apology accepted," said Kim.

"Is my brother asleep?"

"Yeah, but I'll go get him. Have you met him

before?" When no one responded, she said, "Never mind, I'll go get him." She left out.

"Can you say 'doghouse'?" Angie teased.

Dip smacked her on her butt and Donna laughed.

* * *

Red not only started to take care of his African girl, but he gave her money to send to her family in Africa. He also convinced her to stop prostituting. He even moved her out of the apartment she shared with her host family out in Green Meadows. He didn't believe her when she told him she won her visa in a lottery. She worked in a wig shop downtown, but he made her quit that as well.

"In me country you get cocaine $2,000 to $3,000 for an entire kilo," Ngosa informed him one day.

Red laughed, thinking she had no idea what she was talking about. "This is a kilo, baby, not this." He pointed at the two different weights.

It was Ngosa's time to laugh. "In me country, I see thousands of kilos stacked up." She used her pinky nail, filled it with coke, and snorted it into both nostrils. "A hundred times better too."

He let it go then, knowing that he had some grade-A shit. Then things changed after a single image.

Ngosa was on her computer talking to her family in Zambia, something she did daily now that Red sent over two Dell laptops. He was chilling, trying to figure out where he was going to re-up once the twenty-two keys were gone. His four were nearly gone, and he'd talked to Dip about finding another connect. He was as surprised as everyone when LaRon's charges were dropped. Talk on the streets of him maybe snitching ended as fast as it began. The real snitches turning up dead in the streets put the nigga's street rep on another level. He'd gone up against the feds and won.

But LaRon decided he was out, and because he knew the feds were watching him, he told Dip he wanted no part in anything illegal. Finding a connect that could supply what they needed wasn't easy.

"Look," Ngosa said one afternoon.

Red got up from the kitchen table where he'd been counting money, and went to where she sat with her laptop. He looked at the screen, waved at the girl he recognized as one of her cousins, and then his eyes got big as the image changed. He took the laptop off her lap and stared at the screen in disbelief. "Is this real?"

They had video and voice activated, so the

cousin nine thousand miles away in Africa heard him, and it was her voice that said, "Real and whatever you want."

The camera built into the laptop circled the inside of the hut that was filled with cocaine, heroin, pills, and exotic mushrooms. Every area was labeled with a simple piece of paper, with a handwritten word of the drug it was in front of.

Red's mind began to work. If he could line up a connect and spend what Ngosa said one would cost, he could make a killing. He handed her back her computer. "We need to talk."

It was on that day that he found a connect that could supply his crew with more than what they required. A month later after taking all the required tests, getting a visa, and taking the medications needed to fight off all foreign bacteria, Red made the first of many trips to Africa.

What he discovered was it wasn't all jungle and people wore clothes and drove cars just like back home.

The first shipment was fifty kilos flown over to Canada by a private plane. From there, it was brought across the border into New York. Red caught a Continental flight to JFK in New York. He picked up the fifty keys from an African. It was a simple matter from there to Pittsburgh, all accomplished for $150,000. The price he paid for everything was way cheaper than if he got it in the States. It was more potent too.

TWENTY

For A.D., everything was different. With his girl having a son, Joel having one of each, and his thriving drug dealing, he stayed busy. Nothing seemed the same though. The saying, "You never miss a good thing until it's gone," rang true in the case of Joel being gone. There weren't too many days that went past that A.D. didn't think about him. He visited Joel's mom and siblings often. There was nothing Sasha and Maria needed that he didn't get. When he had Taylor start an account for his unborn son, he had her open two for Joel's kids. Being able to make the type of money the two friends often dreamed of, he wondered what Joel would have done. He talked to both Maria and Sasha and learned of Joel's change of decision about having kids. He was glad and couldn't wait until they were born. Maria, who was having his son, already said she was going to name him "Joel Jr."

* * *

After six months, the four members controlled much of the city's drug trade. It was just as Dip planned it, but with Red's African connect, and the cheap cost, even Dip was surprised at how much paper they were stacking.

"We got to wash this money somehow," Red told the other three bosses.

When they got into it, none of them thought they'd be making the type of money they were so quickly. There had been no talk of washing the money. Dip was the only one who had legitimate money coming in through his rental properties.

The four had a meeting every week to talk about the areas they covered. It was also time to show the books that each kept. Although there was no boss, Dip was the one who made sure the money and product matched week in and week out. There were also payouts that had to be dished out to members of the police force. In each zone they operated in, they had an inside connect that kept them on point with raids, warrants, and lost evidence when it got that far.

Sometimes they had to let their guns handle the negotiation when their words to niggas who didn't want to follow the program weren't enough. Bodies popped up, but by the sixth month, things settled as word spread of what was later to be known as the "New Fam."

"Tomorrow, I want each of you to bring me

$250,000. I got someone who is going to start washing it," Dip told them.

Red and A.D. immediately agreed, but Sean who handled the North side, didn't.

"My people is already on top of things." He'd gotten out of the game awhile ago, but frequent trips to casinos, vacations, and high-priced living depleted his nest egg that he had accumulated over the years as a major drug dealer. "Dre got me hooked up."

They all knew who Andre was. He was the one nigga that once had the crack game on lock. No one outside of his family knew the reason for him getting out, but one day he just did. It was estimated that he walked away with over $100 million. Sean was once on his team. He too had no idea how much Andre had, but there was once a rumor he was attempting to buy the Pittsburgh Pirates.

Dip had considered going to Dre himself, but his wife had a cousin in New York that worked on Wall Street. She was a serious investor and knew what she was doing. Her only requirement was her identity was to be hidden from everyone but Dip himself. The money also had to be delivered by him in person, and never anyone else. He thought it all a little extreme, but he went along with it.

* * *

With the birth of his son a month away, A.D. and Taylor got married. It almost didn't take place as Taylor, eight months pregnant, thought she looked like a stuffed pig in her white lace gown.

"All I need is a bright red apple in my mouth."

A.D. laughed, "You ain't even that big."

She punched him in his stomach. "What the hell is that supposed to mean? I ain't that big, but I'm big. That's it, I'm not getting married until after I have the baby and I'm back to a size 7."

They were at her family's house having dinner. Everyone around the table was laughing, but Taylor didn't think anything was funny.

"You ain't been a 7 since middle school," her older sister teased.

"At least," her mother agreed.

Taylor burst out in tears. "I hate all of you!"

If there was a Guinness record for worst mom to be for emotional, uncalled, outbursts, Taylor would have won it hands down. If she didn't cry at least once a day, A.D. asked her if she was okay. No one paid her any mind as she cried, not even A.D., who was focused on his food.

"Y'all don't even care I'll be wobbling down the aisle."

"You'll waddle, honey, not wobble," her aunt

pointed out.

The aunt was actually a year younger than she was, and the two were very close. "Waddle, wobble. Bitch, you know what I mean. I won't be walking right."

More laughter.

She hit A.D. on his arm. 'It's all your fault I'm fat."

"Stop hitting on that boy," her mom said. "Should have hit him long before now. Maybe you wouldn't be pregnant."

Taylor picked off his plate. Her mood changed and she smiled. "Pass the dessert."

* * *

Joel's dad was A.D.'s best man when he got married. Both Joel and A.D. had said they'd never get married. If his bro was there, A.D. joked that they probably would have had a double wedding.

"Yeah," his dad said. "He would have had Sasha on one arm and Maria on the other."

A.D. agreed. The wedding was a joyful moment for the four bosses—a time to celebrate and kick back. They had no worries that day.

Unfortunately, the days and weeks to follow were another story . .

TWENTY-ONE

LaRon still had his eyes and ears on the streets. Saying you are finished and actually carrying it out are two different things. He got word how Dip and his New Fam crew had shit on lock. With his third child being born, and nothing to do all day, LaRon got bored—bored enough to take up golf, a sport he once refused to classify as a sport. He even got Dip interested in it, and the two used their Sunday morning rounds out at North Hills Range as a means to talk and catch up.

Dip was about to tee off at the eighth hole. It was only a 230-yard hole, a par 3, but Dip was no Tiger. He wasn't even LaRon. If he hit a triple bogey, that was a minor miracle. "Bend your knees, homie," LaRon instructed.

He wasn't above direction, so he did as he was told. He hit the ball cleanly, but it sailed a good hundred yards past the hole. "That's some bullshit."

LaRon laughed. "Every hole ain't 400 yards, nigga. Take something off." He approached his tee, placed his ball, and settled himself. His swing was just as clean as Dip's, but with less power. The ball soared and settled on the green. If his putting game was right, he'd birdie the hole, but he struggled with that part of his game. What just happened reminded him of something he needed to talk to Dip about. "It's the same with the streets, homie. Sometimes muscle is called for, and other times finesse. That kid getting shot was too much muscle."

The incident LaRon referred to had happened three days previous. One of Dip's crew banged at some niggas that was hustling on the block on some renegade shit: "It ain't our shit you hustling, you won't be doing no hustling."

LaRon understood the law they were laying down, but not the way it was handled. With so many bodies over the spring and summer, the heat was already coming down from the mayor and chief of police. A drug and gang task force had hit the city, and you had to be on your toes. The Code of Silence ruled every hood, but the killing of young, innocent kids brought unwanted heat and attention. When you had people in the hood appearing on the news saying they were fed up, you had to use finesse. The child shot was a seven-year-old girl.

Dip nodded in agreement. "I know her older sister and some other family members."

They couldn't bring the little girl back, but they could seal some loose lips. "What I suggest is you cover the cost of her funeral, take care of her family, and have a community event in her honor."

"And the nigga who spanked her?"

LaRon stepped on the green and set up for his birdie putt. It was maybe seventeen feet from the hole. He connected smoothly with the ball. It stopped on the edge of the hole, and then as if the wind added it, it dropped in the hole. LaRon pumped his fist as he'd seen Tiger do on numerous occasions. He retrieved the ball and tossed it in the air as he said, "Get rid of him."

If there was a don of the New Fam, it was made that day on the North Hills Golf Course.

Any major decisions from that day forward were first cleared by LaRon before a move was made. Only Dip was aware of LaRon's involvement.

* * *

A.D. had waited on this day to arrive. He would finally able to get the niggas back who were responsible for killing Joel. The dumb niggas had actually bragged about killing a boss of the New Fam. When word got back to Red, he immediately gave A.D. the heads up. It had taken almost seven months, but he had names, addresses, and photos of the two niggas claiming responsibility. A.D. immediately recognized one of the niggas. He knew his boy wasn't well liked and had a lot of enemies.

But to find out Joel was killed by the nigga from Sandcastle hurt. He couldn't help but take some of the blame. If it weren't for him catching feelings, they wouldn't have gotten into it with the four niggas—two of which survived that day. They survived only to kill Joel, and for that, both niggas must die.

A.D. knew nothing about Duquesne. He hit high rollers out in Homestead and the 801 out in McKeesport, but those were the only areas out in Mon Valley that he kicked it at. He had all he needed to know. It was a little after six in the evening when he reached the street one of the niggas lived on. It was the one that tried to talk to his woman at the time, now his wife. That added more fuel to the fire. He thought about taking the chopper to him, but after the Fam's weekly talk about making sure no innocent lives were taken, he chose the Glock. Since he intended on walking right up on the nigga masked up and wearing his Teflon vest, he parked and got out.

The nigga A.D. was looking for was named Dub D. He was from Hazelwood, but stayed in Duquesne now. He was a hustler, but nothing major. A.D. noticed the limp before he saw the nigga's face. He heard the bullets from the chopper Joel had hit him up with, permanently disfiguring him, and taking out a nice chunk of his hip—the cause for the limp.

Dub D jumped in a car with someone else already inside, and after looking down at the photo, A.D. saw it was the nigga's half-brother. He was only nineteen, but he wouldn't see twenty. Both men had participated in the killing of Joel. The mom they shared would be holding a double funeral—closed caskets. A.D. followed behind them a safe distance, so as not to be detected. He had no idea where they were going. When they headed toward Homestead, he figured they were going to the waterfront. That wasn't the spot to ambush them. Too many cameras, undercovers, and people.

When they headed across the Homestead Bridge, he breathed a sigh of relief. He had no intention of putting off their deaths. Not even if it had to take place at the Waterfront . After they got across the bridge, they stopped at the light and made the left, heading up into Glen Hazel.

"Hello," A.D. said as he answered the phone.

"You busy, baby?" Taylor asked.

"A little, but what's up?" On this back road, he had to let them get a nice lead on him. "Can you bring some butter pecan ice cream home?"

He smiled. He knew she was calling because she wanted something to eat. In a week, their son was due, and he couldn't wait. "I got you, lil mami."

"Love you."

"Love you, baby." He hung up and speed up a

little. They got too far ahead. Up on Johnson Avenue up by the rec center, their car was pulled over. A.D. drove past and saw only the younger brother sitting behind the wheel. His head was down, obviously rolling a blunt.

A.D. pulled over and got out. The skully he had on was actually a mask once you pulled it down. Now wasn't the time. The rec center itself was open, but no one stood out front. He eased up the street seemingly on a walk. He noticed the young nigga look up when he gutted the blunt. Seeing A.D. as no threat, he went back to rolling his blunt. A.D. pulled out a Newport, felt around in his pants pockets, and then approached the car. "You got a light, cuz?"

Russ was about to say naw, but he knew the nigga saw him rolling the blunt. He reached in the center console and got his lighter. "Here," he looked up.

"That nigga you spanked on Carlson was my best friend," A.D. informed the nigga as he pointed the Glock at his face.

Russell was too shocked to say anything. He dropped the half rolled blunt, spilling its contents onto the car floor.

"Where is your strap, nigga?"

"Under my seat." Russell didn't want to die. "Cuz, I'm sorry, cuz. Please don't kill me."

A.D. opened the car door and pulled the nigga

out by his shirt. "I want your brother. Is he in the rec?"

"Yeah."

"When he comes out, you better start laughing," A.D. ordered. The two were basically the same height, so A.D. stood in front of him, facing the center's front door. He used the nigga as a shield so he could face the door without being seen.

It took about five minutes for Dub D to come out, but he wasn't alone. A.D. was past caring.

A.D. saw the nigga stutter step when he saw his brother out of the car.

"Laugh, nigga," he ordered as he pressed the barrel into his stomach.

Russ began to laugh, and Dub D continued to limp toward the car. Dub D's eyes stayed on them though, and his hand began to raise to his waist.

The time was now. A.D. shot Russ in his stomach. It exited his side and shattered the car's windshield. As soon as he pulled the trigger, he was in motion, stepping around the car and emptying his gun into the unsuspecting men. He stood over Dub D and shot him in his face. He was turning to do the same thing to the young nigga, when a bullet hit him right below the vest he had on. He fell back and dropped the gun.

Standing on shaky legs holding the gun he retrieved from under the seat, was Russell.

A.D. struggled to roll over. A shot missed him and then he took one in the chest. The wind was knocked out of him and he lay there waiting on death.

Russell took a final step and then fell.

It seemed like forever but finally A.D. got up to his feet. He picked up his gun, pulled down his mask, and calmly walked over the dead youngster and shot him in the face just as he'd said he would do—closed caskets. He jumped in the young nigga's car 'cause he doubted he could make it to his car. He pulled out and headed down Johnson. He could hear the sirens in the distance. All he had to do was get away. He reached for his phone, realized it was in his car, and then passed out. The car, still moving, crashed into several parked cars before it came to a stop.

A.D. opened up his eyes. He tried to raise his hand to his eyes, and realized he was handcuffed to a bed.

"You have a right to remain silent, anything you say can be used against you in a court of law. Do you understand your rights?"

"What am I charged with?"

"Triple homicide," the cop informed him. A.D. closed his eyes. It was over for him.

Twenty-Two

He wasn't allowed any visitors, outside of his lawyer, in his hospital room. The bullet had hit an artery and A.D. had no idea he almost died when he crashed into the parked cars. He told the cops he had nothing to say and he wanted his attorney. The following day he heard the cops' account of what happened from his attorney. Dip saw the shooting coverage on the news and sent an attorney ASAP.

"You had the gun in your lap, Mr. Davis. The angle we will try to go on is self-defense. It was three against one, and from what I'm hearing, all three were carrying."

It was a small hope, but A.D. wasn't new to the system. He knew shit wasn't fair, and he knew that if he got found guilty, he'd likely be spending the rest of his life behind bars. He couldn't believe he'd been so sloppy and allowed the young nigga to get out on him. He replayed the whole scene over and over again in his head. He should've shot him in the head, should've taken the gun from under the seat, should've used a silencer. There was a whole lot of scenarios he played out in his mind. Now he was laid out in a hospital bed, handcuffed, with a cop right outside of his room. He'd already received word from the detective that once he was well enough, he'd be arraigned and taken to the county jail and placed in the infirmary. He dreamed of escaping, thought that Dip and Red would break him out. Taylor's due date came and went. He worried about her. Finally, his attorney came with news that he had a healthy son and his wife was fine. He even snuck a picture of his son in on one visit, but he didn't want to leave it with A.D.

A.D. continued to think of Joel. Since his death, everything had been slowly going downhill. He wished he was here now. He needed him. When he went to sleep that night, he had a nightmare, one in which he was sentenced to death. He woke up sweating, just as the doctor was administering the lethal dose.

"A nightmare?" the cop asked. Usually he was outside the door, but the rattling and tossing and turning A.D. was doing caused him to come into the room.

"Yeah, what time is it?"

"4:30 a.m."

He moved the bed up by pushing a button, "I'm pretty much done, huh?"

Keith Washington had pulled hospital duty

because he was in the doghouse with the captain. He was an eight year police officer. He'd seen open and shut cases before. None like this one. "I think so."

A.D. sat there a long moment. He wanted out, wanted to see his wife and son. Damn, he thought, why had Joel let himself be killed? A tear rolled down his cheek. "How can I get out of this?"

He'd sat in on his share of interrogations before. He knew the routine. A triple homicide was major. "You'd have to have some valuable info that could make the murders go away."

More tears fell. He hated himself for what he was about to do. "Ever heard of the New Fam?"

Keith had, and he also knew an investigation was about to be conducted on it. "Keep going."

"I'm a boss of the New Fam. I can bring them all down."

"Stop." This was enough and big enough to wake up the captain.

* * *

A.D. sat up, looking at the head of the FBI Agency and Chief of Police of Pittsburgh. The two men had been awakened from their sleep at 5:00 a.m. They now sat in the hospital room, and it was a little after 6:00 a.m.

Besides the two of them, Ofc. Washington, Capt. Ambrosso, and a federal DA all waited for A.D. to begin. A tape recorder sat on the portable counter in front of him. He looked down at it as the spools began to spin.

After a minute, A.D. waved his hand causing the DA to stop the recorder. "What is it?"

"Some of the things I'm about to tell you I participated in. I won't be charged with them too will I?"

"Mr. Davis," the FBI agent, named Albert Haynes, began. "If your info leads to the arrest of the reputed drug bosses of the New Fam, then you'd be granted immunity. You'll also be afforded the opportunity to go into the Witness Protection Program." Agent Haynes was drawing the ire of the director in Washington over the influx of homicides in the city. He wanted the killers brought to justice. A covert investigation was just about to be launched against them: not only the gangs in the city, but also drug lords and mafia. He'd nearly lost his job when a breach within his office and ranks caused the death of a man under their protection. A federal lawsuit had just been filed by the man's family and he'd be forced to settle that quickly. This would put him back in the good graces of the director.

"Are you ready?" the DA asked.

A.D. took a deep breath and nodded. The DA pushed the start button. "Can you please state your birth date and name for the record?"

"Anthony Davis. September 6, 1983."

"So that makes you twenty-four, Mr. Davis?"

"Yes."

"Is it by your own accord that you wish to reveal information that will lead to the arrest of the head men of the New Fam, a drug ring here in the city of Pittsburgh?"

Time ticked as A.D. fought the demons within himself. He'd lived by the hood code of no snitching his entire life, a code as strong as the Los Costa Masters' stance on rats. He knew once he crossed the unthinkable line, his name would be mud on the streets, and his life in jeopardy.

"Mr. Davis, did you hear me?" the DA asked impatiently.

"Yeah." As he nodded, he thought of Taylor and his son whom he hadn't held yet. "It's deeper than even y'all realize. Cops are being paid off to look the other way and reveal info."

"Wait a minute," the chief interjected, but he was waved off by the DA.

A.D. looked at the man. "Do y'all want it all or do y'all just want the New Fam?"

"We want it all, but can we start with the names

of the New Fam bosses?"

"Okay. There's Roger 'Dipset' Underwild; Jared 'Red' Thomason; Joel, who was my best friend but was killed by the men I killed up Hazelwood; and a nigga named Sean, from the North side. I don't know his last name, and myself. Us five started it all."

"Started it all. Elaborate on that, please."

A.D. smiled. "We controlled the drug trade in the city of Pittsburgh. We covered each side— North, South, East and West. If you weren't selling our shit, you weren't selling shit. And if you did, you got dealt with."

"Dealt with?"

"Might be a beatdown at first, a shot in the leg or something small. But if you continued, we killed you or had someone kill you."

"So is it your testimony that the members of the New Fam ordered and participated in the killings of rivals?"

"Yeah. Even a few cops carried out executions. Remember the cop shooting of the dude in Homewood? Said the boy went for his gun?"

The DA shook his head from side to side indicating no.

"Cop killed him 'cuz Dip gave the order. He wanted to seal the cop's loyalty and kill the nigga that hit his baby sister."

"Wait, wait, wait," the DA interrupted. "Let's start from the beginning. How was the New Fam formed?"

"From twenty-two kilos of cocaine given to Dip by a nigga named LaRon."

"LaRon Jones?" the DA said. He couldn't' contain his excitement. "Is he involved in this?"

"No. He got out of the game. Dip got robbed for his stash and got back in. LaRon gave Dip all the coke he had in a bank in Oakland."

The DA had thought the cocaine in the bank story was bullshit. Now he knew that it wasn't. He also knew he'd get LaRon. He'd tie him in there somehow. "Keep talking, Mr. Davis."

Talk he did. For days, unbeknownst to anyone in the New Fam, he told on them told everything. As fast as it began, it fell. Three hundred and forty-seven members would be indicted in the largest sting the city had ever seen.

From that moment on, anyone snitching would be classified as "giving up A.D. tapes."

Twenty-Three

L aRon, with his wife and kids at his side, stood in a line that stretched down and around the block. People talked excitedly. No one truly believed this day would come. Old black men and women in their sixties, seventies, and eighties who witnessed and suffered during the Jim Crow laws were out casting their votes—many voting for the first time in their lives. Drug dealers, business owners, gang bangers, blue collar workers, nine to fivers, blacks out in mass numbers.

People from ages eighteen to ninety-eight stood out in the chilly morning air to vote for Barack Obama. A black man, running for president of the United States. No one could believe it. That he wasn't killed by now was a major miracle in itself. That he actually had a chance to beat John McCain was beyond a miracle.

LaRon and Deamber were first-time voters. Neither had any previous knowledge of anything political. They got caught up in the mania that now surrounded this presidency run.

"If he made Hillary vice president, this wouldn't

even be a race," an older lady said. "Everyone knows and loves Hillary Clinton. If not her, then definitely Bill Clinton."

Several people agreed. Bill Clinton was loved by a lot of blacks. "Who is Joe Biden?"

"He's gonna win no matter what," one man predicted.

"Let's just hope they don't pull that shit they pulled in Florida all around the country."

LaRon had no idea what the man was talking about. He thought Obama was going to win. He felt it in his bones.

"Can I vote, Dad?" his namesake asked.

"Too young, Son, but one day you'll be able to tell your kids and grandkids that you were there, that you stood in line with your parents while they voted for Obama—the first black president of the United States.

Those who heard him nodded their heads in agreement. On this day, there was no killing, and surprisingly, hardly any drug selling around the country. There was just a profound love of being black and thankful to be partaking in this historical event.

India voted that day as well, taking along her little sisters, and Clyde, who now got around with little discomfort. The two were now an official couple, and India was no longer a virgin.

The two were very much in love.

The New Fam bosses voted that chilly day in November 2007 along with the members of their organization. They even campaigned in the neighborhoods for Obama, making sure people could get to and from the poll booths, by hiring a fleet of school buses. This would be their last good deed as an organization. In days it would all be dismantled.

TWENTY-FOUR

The high he felt after watching the coverage of Barack Obama win the election carried on after the final announcement at 9:00 p.m. People celebrated long into the night. Dip had put his kids to sleep and was lying in the bed with his wife. They'd just finished making love.

"Didn't Michelle look beautiful in all that red?" Kim asked. Being a black woman herself, she took pride in the fact that the First Lady was a black woman.

He smiled. "Got a bubble."

Kim hit him playfully in his chest. "You would notice that."

"Ain't knockin' yours, but she's working with a little something."

She couldn't hate on the wife of Barack Obama. Michelle had it going on. "Hopefully this changes shit."

That was still to be seen. It was baby steps now. At least they now literally had their foot in the door.

Kim screamed as a loud explosion rocked the downstairs. Their bay window exploded as a man clad in black propelled himself through the glass. A red dot from the laser beam on the AR-15 then pointed at Dip. It was dead center on his chest.

"FBI. Don't move!" the man ordered.

Dip held onto his scared and naked wife. He'd talked to Red and asked him if A.D. would stand up. He was told that he probably would, but that anything could happen. He considered attempting to kill him, but had put it off. Now he regretted doing that.

More FBI agents entered their bedroom. One was guiding his screaming son into the room.

"Mr. Roger Underwood, you are under arrest and being indicted under the RICO Act. You are being charged with numerous drug code violations and murder in the 1st degree amongst other crimes"

Dip knew then that they had it all. A.D. must have told them everything. His run had come to an end.

They pulled him out of bed naked, and he was thankful they didn't do the same thing to his wife. He got dressed, and with one last look at his wife, they led him out.

"Tear this place apart," one agent ordered.

LaRon was rounded up that night, as well as India. Although he wasn't labeled a member of the New Fam, LaRon started it off by turning over the twenty-two keys.

Arrested for the first time in her life, India saw firsthand what it was like. Her charges were simple—receiving the money from Dip for payment of the kilos. She was granted bond, but her brother wasn't.

Fannie Oliver was re-arrested. Twice in a month was too much for her. She went against her husband and became a witness for the feds.

All across the city, members were getting caught and placed in the Allegheny County Jail. Sean, a New Fam member, attempted to fight his way out of his home. He was shot twice and would survive.

Red, the remaining boss, managed to escape from the feds as they attempted to pull his 'Vette over. He caused several vehicle accidents that day, but got away on foot as he abandoned the damaged $125,000 car. The last anyone heard from him was later that day as he vowed that he would never sit in a prison. He'd rather die first.

Dip received life as did Sean. LaRon got a federal sentence of 36 months and 5 years' probation for his participation. India only got 2 years' probation and the loss of her legal license. Others, including cops, attorneys, political figures, and New Fam members, got sentences of 5 to 135 years, depending on their charges.

TOMORROW'S NOT PROMISED 2

It was officially the end of the New Fam organization. Now they all got a taste of the Flip Side of the game.

EPILOGUE

By the time 2010 came in, everyone forgot about the New Fam organization. Although no one attempted to rule the entire city's drug game as New Fam managed to do, more hustlers settled in their hoods and picked up where New Fam had left off—chasing that mighty dollar.

A.D. hid out after he took the stand. He convinced Taylor to join him under federal protection. It wasn't easy because they'd never come back to their old life ever again—not even to visit their families. After three years, A.D. got tired of the control the feds had over his life. In accordance with his plea, he had to turn over $2.5 million dollars. He had a new identity and even a job, but it wasn't the life he wanted. He snitched to be with his family. He didn't give a fuck who went down. What he wasn't was a bitch. He wasn't going to run any more. He signed himself out of Witness Protection, along with his family. Against the fed's advice, he returned to Pittsburgh—a huge mistake. Someone hadn't forgot and never stopped looking for him.

A.D. regretted returning to Pittsburgh. He sat tied in a chair knowing that whoever snatched him, would kill him. He didn't have long to wait to see who was going to kill him. When the figure began to walk toward him, he could not believe his eyes. "You."

India smiled. "Who did you expect, Satan? You fuckin' snitch! Did you think you'd get away with snitching?" She walked behind him.

A.D. didn't have time to think. His head was pulled back and his throat was sliced with the straight razor India held in her hand. He fell to the floor.

"Can you hang his body from the West End Bridge?" India said.

"Consider it done," Mike Astari said. He still held out hope that one day India would be his.

India thanked him, dropped the razor and gloves, and walked out. Her brother would be home in a week. She finally felt like it was over.

Or was it?

BONUS READ

With the death of her husband, Taylor's immediate reaction was fear. The decision to go into the Witness Protection Program wasn't an easy one to make. Not only because of the fact she'd never get to visit with her family again, but also because of A.D.'s choice to turn a snitch. She wasn't ghetto, but she came up in the streets. She knew the street laws, and at the head of those laws was no snitching.

When she'd received word from an agent in the FBI that A.D. was telling, she was infuriated. She would have much rather had him die in a hail of bullets. At least then she could walk around with her head held high. Being labeled the BM to the nigga who brought an entire organization down wasn't the recognition she wanted for herself.

For days, she stayed in her apartment, ignoring calls from A.D. and the FBI.

"I did it for you."

The words jarred her out of her sleep. She sat up with a start, her heart racing.

A.D. sat at the bottom of her bed, near her feet. He watched her sleep for some time before he spoke.

She heard his words and knew they weren't true. He told to save his own ass. For a long moment, the two just sat and looked at each other.

"I did it for you," he repeated.

"You did it for yourself! Don't try to use me as an excuse."

When he got word that Taylor didn't want anything to do with him, he couldn't believe it and refused to accept it. He informed the director that all deals were off if he couldn't see her.

Albert Haynes thought with the info he had, he could get a conviction without Anthony Davis testifying in court. It made his case stronger with him, and that is the only reason he gave the okay to the late night visit.

"You can't face the music, Anthony. You cracked when the cuffs clicked on." She said this not as a taunt; just for what it was—the truth.

He'd beat himself up enough over his decision to snitch. His old way of life was over for him. That much he did know. He had no other out. Tell or spend the rest of his life behind bars. He cried as he sat there and stared at the woman he loved. She'd met the top niggas he fucked with, even some of his crew he ran with. She didn't understand the ruthlessness the niggas possessed, the measures they'd go to if they couldn't get the one they wanted. He was one of them. He knew what he'd do: get someone close to the nigga. In his case, it was his wife and newborn son. He reached into his pocket and removed the photos he requested from the agent, brutal photos showing the lifeless bodies of the men who went up against the New Fam and paid with their lives. He laid them on her lap.

She couldn't help but see them. Knocking them off her lap, she attacked her husband, hating him for what he'd done and for putting her life and their son's life in jeopardy.

He didn't defend himself, allowing her to hit him in his chest and face.

Two agents rushed in and managed to pull her off of him. Blood trickled from his busted lip. His son awakened from the noise and began to cry. A.D. stood up.

Taylor hated him. Hated him for what he'd done. She shrugged off the agent's hand and went to her son's room. She had no choice but to go into hiding.

"Ma'am, I believe it best if you accept our protection," one agent said.

"I'll accept, but not with my husband." She couldn't deal with him and didn't know if she ever could.

For ten months, she kept her distance, wanting nothing to do with her husband.

Phoenix, Arizona, is where she made her home. Not being able to call her family and friends ate at her. All alone, she finally gave in to her husband and the two were reunited.

Now after three years, Taylor sat in front of her TV emotionless. A.D.'s body hanging from the West End Bridge was on the Channel 11 breaking news.

"In a gruesome discovery just a half hour ago, the body of a twenty-seven-year-old black male, who police have identified as Anthony David from the West side, was discovered by a passing boat. Mr. David, was a central part . . ."

Taylor turned off the TV as her son came into her room in his pajamas. She knew the entire story. She'd lived it.

"Mommy, where Daddy at?"

She pulled her son up onto her lap and held him tight. "Ant, Mommy got something to tell you . . ." It was then that she told Anthony Jr. that his dad wouldn't be coming back home—that he was in heaven.

Her son wiped at her tears. "Don't cry, Mommy. Jesus is in heaven. So is Nanna."

Her mother died of breast cancer in 2009. She wasn't crying because A.D. was dead. The love she had once had for him was long gone. Her tears were for her son, who would grow up without a father. Hearing his words, she realized he'd be just fine.

Text Good2Go at 31996 to receive new release updates via text message.

To order books, please fill out the order form below:
To order films please go to www.good2gofilms.com

Name:_____

Address:_____

City: _____ State: _____ Zip Code: _____

Phone:_____

Email:_____

Method of Payment: Check   VISA   MASTERCARD

Credit Card#:_____

Name as it appears on card: _____

Signature: _____

Item Name	Price	Qty	Amount
48 Hours to Die – Silk White	$14.99		
A Hustler's Dream - Ernest Morris	$14.99		
A Hustler's Dream 2 - Ernest Morris	$14.99		
Black Reign – Ernest Morris	$14.99		
Bloody Mayhem Down South	$14.99		
Business Is Business – Silk White	$14.99		
Business Is Business 2 – Silk White	$14.99		
Business Is Business 3 – Silk White	$14.99		
Childhood Sweethearts – Jacob Spears	$14.99		
Childhood Sweethearts 2 – Jacob Spears	$14.99		
Childhood Sweethearts 3 - Jacob Spears	$14.99		
Childhood Sweethearts 4 - Jacob Spears	$14.99		
Connected To The Plug – Dwan Marquis Williams	$14.99		
Connected To The Plug 2 – Dwan Marquis Williams	$14.99		
Connected To The Plug 2 – Dwan Williams	$14.99		
Deadly Reunion – Ernest Morris	$14.99		
Flipping Numbers – Ernest Morris	$14.99		
Flipping Numbers 2 – Ernest Morris	$14.99		
He Loves Me, He Loves You Not - Mychea	$14.99		
He Loves Me, He Loves You Not 2 - Mychea	$14.99		
He Loves Me, He Loves You Not 3 - Mychea	$14.99		
He Loves Me, He Loves You Not 4 – Mychea	$14.99		
He Loves Me, He Loves You Not 5 – Mychea	$14.99		
Lord of My Land – Jay Morrison	$14.99		
Lost and Turned Out – Ernest Morris	$14.99		
Married To Da Streets – Silk White	$14.99		
M.E.R.C. - Make Every Rep Count Health and Fitness	$14.99		

Money Make Me Cum – Ernest Morris	$14.99		
My Besties – Asia Hill	$14.99		
My Besties 2 – Asia Hill	$14.99		
My Besties 3 – Asia Hill	$14.99		
My Besties 4 – Asia Hill	$14.99		
My Boyfriend's Wife - Mychea	$14.99		
My Boyfriend's Wife 2 – Mychea	$14.99		
My Brothers Envy – J. L. Rose	$14.99		
My Brothers Envy 2 – J. L. Rose	$14.99		
Naughty Housewives – Ernest Morris	$14.99		
Naughty Housewives 2 – Ernest Morris	$14.99		
Naughty Housewives 3 – Ernest Morris	$14.99		
Naughty Housewives 4 – Ernest Morris	$14.99		
Never Be The Same – Silk White	$14.99		
Stranded – Silk White	$14.99		
Slumped – Jason Brent	$14.99		
Supreme & Justice – Ernest Morris	$14.99		
Supreme & Justice 2 – Ernest Morris	$14.99		
Supreme & Justice 3 – Ernest Morris	$14.99		
Tears of a Hustler - Silk White	$14.99		
Tears of a Hustler 2 - Silk White	$14.99		
Tears of a Hustler 3 - Silk White	$14.99		
Tears of a Hustler 4- Silk White	$14.99		
Tears of a Hustler 5 – Silk White	$14.99		
Tears of a Hustler 6 – Silk White	$14.99		
The Panty Ripper - Reality Way	$14.99		
The Panty Ripper 3 – Reality Way	$14.99		
The Solution – Jay Morrison	$14.99		
The Teflon Queen – Silk White	$14.99		
The Teflon Queen 2 – Silk White	$14.99		
The Teflon Queen 3 – Silk White	$14.99		
The Teflon Queen 4 – Silk White	$14.99		
The Teflon Queen 5 – Silk White	$14.99		
The Teflon Queen 6 - Silk White	$14.99		

The Vacation – Silk White	$14.99		
Tied To A Boss - J.L. Rose	$14.99		
Tied To A Boss 2 - J.L. Rose	$14.99		
Tied To A Boss 3 - J.L. Rose	$14.99		
Tied To A Boss 4 - J.L. Rose	$14.99		
Tied To A Boss 5 - J.L. Rose	$14.99		
Time Is Money - Silk White	$14.99		
Tomorrow's Not Promised – Robert Torres	$14.99		
Tomorrow's Not Promised 2 – Robert Torres	$14.99		
Two Mask One Heart – Jacob Spears and Trayvon Jackson	$14.99		
Two Mask One Heart 2 – Jacob Spears and Trayvon Jackson	$14.99		
Two Mask One Heart 3 – Jacob Spears and Trayvon Jackson	$14.99		
Wrong Place Wrong Time – Silk White	$14.99		
Young Goonz – Reality Way	$14.99		
Subtotal:			
Tax:			
Shipping (Free) U.S. Media Mail:			
Total:			

Make Checks Payable To:
Good2Go Publishing
7311 W Glass Lane,
Laveen, AZ 85339